Joseph's Journey

MARGARET SANSALONE

Bloomington, IN Milton Keynes, UK

authorHOUSE®

AuthorHouse™
1663 Liberty Drive, Suite 200
Bloomington, IN 47403
www.authorhouse.com
Phone: 1-800-839-8640

AuthorHouse™ UK Ltd.
500 Avebury Boulevard
Central Milton Keynes, MK9 2BE
www.authorhouse.co.uk
Phone: 08001974150

This book is a work of fiction. People, places, events, and situations are the product of the author's imagination. Any resemblance to actual persons, living or dead, or historical events, is purely coincidental.

First published by AuthorHouse 8/28/2007

ISBN: 978-1-4259-9459-4 (sc)

Library of Congress Control Number: 2007900675

Printed in the United States of America
Bloomington, Indiana

This book is printed on acid-free paper.

FOREWORD

Many years ago when I was a little girl, my Aunt Florence was cleaning out her attic. She found an old diary. It was in an old trunk that was full of dusty, old clothes and tin-type pictures. The diary was hand written on yellow legal size paper. It was written in pencil and some of the words had been erased by time. It was the story of our family's journey to Indiana by covered wagon. The author of the diary was my great-grandfather's brother. This book is loosely based on that diary. I have changed the names and created my own adventures for the family. Many of the events that take place in the book are the actual events that Joseph and his family experienced as they moved west.

I hope that you enjoy Joseph's journey.

CHAPTER ONE

Secrets

In his dreams, Joseph Harding heard voices speaking in hushed tones. Emerging from the fog of sleep he leaned over and listened to the quiet snoring noises of his brothers, John and William.

"It's not them talking in their sleep," he said, "and it's the middle of the night so who is it?" Joseph eased out of his bed. Carefully, he moved an arm off of his shoulder and a leg off of his leg. His brothers were apt to roll all over him in their sleep. After slipping out of his room, he closed the door and walked out into the upstairs hall. The voices were louder now and came from the downstairs hall.

Curious, Joseph carefully peeked over the stair railing. He tip-toed closer to the head of the stairway cautiously avoiding the floorboards that creaked and would give him away. Tucking his pale, skinny legs under his nightshirt he crouched down and squatted, hoping not to be seen as he peered between the stairwells. He was shivering as much from nervousness as being chilly. Father and Mother were talking quietly in the hallway below. Since he was small for almost ten, and very thin; he could often make himself almost invisible. He hoped he was unseen right now. He didn't want Mother or Father to see him. They were talking quietly with their heads bent together. Father's head nodded in agreement with what Mother was saying.

"Yes, I agree." Father said. "We must take them with us or they will be sold separately."

Joseph leaned over the railing as far as he could. What were they talking about? Who was coming with them on their journey west? he asked himself. In his excitement, he moved and the floor creaked noisily.

Father looked up at the noise and saw Joseph, who didn't move quickly enough into the shadows.

"Joseph!" he said sternly. "You get back to bed. You'll be too tired for school in the morning."

"Father, who is coming with us on our journey to Indiana?" Joseph ignored his father's order and ran quickly down the stairs.

Father put an arm around Joseph and drew him closer to the fireplace in the parlor. "Joseph, if I tell you, you must keep this a secret. This is not a boy's game. Do I have your word?"

Joseph drew himself up to his full height of four feet and seven and one-half inches and said seriously, "Father, I am almost ten years old. I wouldn't ever tell." He crossed his heart and his deep blue eyes looked solemnly into his father's serious stare.

Father looked into Joseph's eyes and nodded. "As you know, your mother and I are strongly against slavery," Father said. "That is the main reason that we are leaving Virginia. We are being pressured to own slaves and we will not do it. We are going to Indiana because it is a free state. Your Uncle Ike has written us that the land is good and we will do well there. However, that doesn't answer your question does it son?"

"No sir."

"Joseph, we are taking Moses and Jane with us."

"Oh." Joseph said. He knew Moses well. Moses was a slave who came to help father gather the crops. Joseph liked Moses. Moses always took the time to say hello to the children and talk to them. Moses was a very big man. He thought nothing of carrying the children around on his back. He was a deep brown in color and walked with the dignity of royalty. He had reason. In Africa, his grandfather had been a king. His father was the prince and eventually Moses would have been the king of his province. Moses said that jealous cousins had betrayed his father and grandfather and sold them to slave traders. His father and grandfather died on the slave ship coming to America. Moses felt that they had died of broken hearts. Moses was born shortly after they landed in America and he and his mother were sold to Mr. Kramer. He had been Mr. Kramer's slave all of his life.

Joseph didn't know Mose's wife, Jane, that well. He had seen her once when visiting Mr. Kramer's farm. She was very tiny and frail looking. Her skin was the color of caramel candy and she always wore a handkerchief around her hair.

"Joseph! Are you listening?" Joseph jerked and came out of his daydream. Father continued. "Mr. Kramer is going to sell Moses to a plantation down south. What we are about to do is very dangerous because Moses and Jane belong to Mr. Kramer. We will be stealing his property. If we are caught we will be in trouble with the law. Moses and Jane would be punished. They would most likely be sold far away from each other. Your mother and I feel strongly that Mr. Kramer is wrong. By taking Moses and Jane with us we feel that we are doing the right thing. We'll tell your brothers right before we leave. Now Joseph give your mother a kiss and go to bed and keep silent."

"Yes Father." Joseph promised. He hugged his mother and kissed her on the cheek. "Goodnight," he said as he went back up the stairs. He slipped quietly into the bed that he shared with his brothers and thought about what Father had told him. The whole idea frightened him, but Joseph knew first hand how Father felt about slavery. Recently, he and Father had been coming back from town on the Warden Mountain Road. They saw some slaves chained together at the wrist walking behind a man on horseback. There were three women and four men. Father had clenched his jaw and tightened his grip on the wagon reins. Joseph watched as his father's eyes got darker and shine with pent up anger. Father approached the man on horseback.

"Sir, what are you doing with these people? They can barely move in those chains, and their feet are bleeding from the rocky road."

"These 'er Mr. Jakes's runaway darkies from down near Richmond. I gots to chain them so they won't try 'in run off on me agin. That big buck there almost got away, but He ain't no match for me." The man said as he spit a wad of something onto the road.

The man flicked his whip on the backs of the slaves as if they were horses, and the group went on down the winding, mountain road. The chained men and women stumbled to keep up with him.

"Goldarn slave drover ought to be chained," Father muttered under his breath. "Like to see that fat old geezer walk barefoot down this trail." Father continued to mutter under his breath the rest of the way home.

That same day Father came home and started talking seriously about moving. It was the spring of 1850. This would be a hard decision for the Harding family. Father and Mother talked about the trip a lot. They decided that it was best for their family to start over in another state that did not have slaves.

Joseph lay in his bed staring up at the ceiling thinking about leaving his home. His stomach was in a knot and sadness gripped him. He would miss the craggy, steep hills of western Virginia. Hardy County was beautiful to him. He loved the town of Millerburg ,especially the general store where his Aunt Minna always gave him a licorice stick. He didn't want to leave his grandparents, aunts, uncles, and cousins. Of all the things that Joseph would miss, the ageless oak tree by the river was the one pleasure he didn't want to leave. He had spent many a warm, lazy summer day watching the boats go down the river. He had wondered where they were going and why. But he knew that he always wanted to stay right where he was. Now he was going to be one of those travelers, and it made him sick. He clutched his aching stomach, closed his eyes and willed himself to sleep.

The next morning Joseph watched as his mother served up breakfast to everyone. She moved calmly and gracefully around the kitchen table. Mother was tall and slender. Joseph thought she was very pretty, for a mother.

He listened with worry to what his brothers were saying. The older boys were reading Uncle Ike's letter again. It had arrived yesterday. It had arrived yesterday from Indiana. Uncle Ike was Father's brother. Joseph listened and his stomach became queasy.

"Ike says here that the land in Indiana is black and rich." David, who was seventeen, and built like a tree, began.

"And he says that corn seed sprouts overnight in his fields." Isaac, who was fifteen, continued reading over David's shoulder.

"I'm going to own the biggest farm in the state, and you little brother will be my partner. " David slapped Isaac on the back with happy enthusiasm.

"What about us, David? Can we live on your farm," asked eleven year old John. He pointed to the six boys sitting around the trestle table. All eyes were on David except for Joseph's.

"Sure John. My farm will be so big that it will make all of us rich. What's the matter little brother, don't you want to live on my farm?" David asked the very silent Joseph.

Joseph looked up. David was sitting directly across from him and it was impossible not to answer his question. He cleared his throat.

"I don't want to go. Why can't we just stay here and farm like we've always been doing? I like it here. No one we know is in Indiana. Just Uncle Ike, and I don't know him and neither do you." Joseph looked at his brothers puzzled and surprised faces. "Besides," Joseph argued. "how do you know he's not telling us a story just to get us to come there. Maybe he's lonely and wants some company. Anyway," Joseph continued rashly, "Father could get into terrible trouble and…" Joseph realized he'd been about to tell the secret. He clamped a hand over his mouth just as Mother rapped his head with a wooden, cooking spoon.

"You older boys get outside and help your father. John, you get your little brothers ready for school. Now get!" Everyone scrambled to do his chores. Mother had the *Look* on her face. They all looked at

Joseph with questioning glances. Joseph started to follow John trying to avoid his mother.

" As for you young man, " Mother said grabbing Joseph by his suspenders and pointing her spoon at Joseph she began her lecture, "How dare you call Uncle Ike a storyteller? When we get to Indiana you can apologize to him. I'll remind you. Now, get Mary out of her cradle and tend to her while I get the lunches ready."

Mother went to the pantry to get lunch pails and food as Joseph plodded over to baby Mary's cradle. He loved Mary, but he hated to "tend to her." It was a messy, stinky job and he knew that it was Mother's punishment for almost telling the secret. Mary looked up at him with big, blue eyes. She cooed and gurgled and drooled through her toothless gums. Mary was only six months old. Joseph changed her cloth diaper and rocked her, then he put Mary back into her cradle. He handed her a rag doll that she stuffed into her mouth and began to gum.

"I'm going to get me an Indian when I get to Indiana," eight year old Warren stated as he and his brothers walked the mile to the schoolhouse.

"Me too! I'm going to scalp one!" yelled William, who was six.

Joseph cringed. He always had thought that Willie was bloodthirsty.

"You're both being silly," Joseph began. "You heard Father say that the Indians are peaceful. Most of them were sent west after the French and Indian War. The only Indians left are farmers and hunters. Besides, wanting to go somewhere just so you can kill someone is horrible. You should be ashamed."

Joseph would have gone on, but a look from John silenced him. John always stood up to Joseph if he was preaching to the younger boys. Joseph didn't think he was being mean. He was just setting them straight. Besides, it didn't look like the little ones were convinced. They were chasing each other down the lane whooping and aiming imaginary arrows at each other. John hurried along to catch up to them. Joseph dragged behind hoping to slow time down. Joseph would miss school. Even though the teacher was stern, Joseph loved to learn. He especially loved reading. He couldn't understand why David and Isaac had happily quit school to help Father get the wagon built for their journey west. Even John, who was the closest to Joseph in age and his best friend was anxious for school to be out so that he could help Father.

"Maybe when I'm ten I'll be that way too." He thought. He doubted it. Lost in thought he was startled when a small hand grabbed his larger one. He looked into James's tear filled eyes.

"Everybody lefted us, Joseph. You won't leave me will you?" James asked tearfully.

"Nope." Joseph put an arm around his little brother and smiled at him. Maybe this one would be his ally in his fight to stay. The four year old did like him and James was fiercely loyal to Joseph. "We'd better hurry ,though, or the teacher will thrash us for being late." Joseph and James ran down the dusty lane entering the school yard just as the bell was ringing.

CHAPTER TWO

Plans And Secrets

They were leaving in just two more days. Mother had been cooking and canning food for a week and Father had built the wagon. He and the older boys had attached the canvas top and repaired the harnesses and other tools.

Joseph had a horrible knot in his stomach when he saw the finished wagon.

It's honest to goodness going to happen, and I haven't got a plan yet. Joseph worried as he and his brothers walked to school. They had left Father, David and Issac doing something to the underneath side of the wagon.

"I wonder what Father is doing?" William questioned.

"I dunno." The others responded.

Hmm. Joseph thought to himself. I wonder if it has something to do with Moses and Jane? I know! I could tell Mr. Kramer what Father is planning and then…no, that would just get Father into lots of trouble. Joseph felt ashamed of that idea. Besides, I want to help Moses too. Why couldn't we all just stay here? Moses doesn't seem that unhappy. Joseph reasoned to himself. He continued to think silently until his brother's talking invaded his thoughts.

"I hate to go to school when I could be helping Father, Isaac, and David get ready." John complained as he and his younger brothers walked the dirt lane to the schoolhouse.

" I know what you mean John, but Father says we have to get all the learning we can because there may not be a school in Indiana." Warren scratched a mosquito bite on his arm and continued, "besides, we only have another day and we'll be helping Father and David pack up the wagon. I can hardly wait to go, but I'll miss Gran and Uncle John Bly."

"I'll miss Gran's pies a lot." James cried, "She makes the best apple pies I ever ate." James began to cry with gusto and wiped his chubby cheeks, streaking them with dirt and tears.

"Now stop that James. You're almost five years old. You are too old to be a crybaby. Come'n boys or we'll be late and Ole' Mr. Brown'll yell at us." John, the eldest of the four, pulled James by the hand, and the others ran as they heard the school bell ringing. Joseph hurried too, for he eagerly looked forward to school. Seeing James cry made him want to cry too, but the others would think him a bawlbaby. He was too old to cry even though he felt like bursting into tears.

Mother came out of the house carrying baby Mary in her arms. She looked for her husband but instead saw Ben Singer. Samuel had hired him to help them on their journey.

"Ben," she asked, "do you know where my husband is?"

No ma'am , I don't. David is in the barn and Isaac is out in the field getting the horses. "

"Thank you Ben." Mother said as she went back into the house to finish her packing. After she put the same towel in three different places she gave in to her worries. She knew Samuel must be going to get Moses and Jane from the woods. They had been hiding there for two days and it was time to bring them up to the house. Mr. Kramer had already been nosing around looking for Moses. Father had hired Moses and Jane for a week to help them get ready to pack. Then, they would pretend to go to Grandmother Bly's house to help her get her spring cleaning done. Mr. Kramer seemed very suspicious and kept hanging around.

Father brought Moses out one day when Mr. Kramer was lurking.

"There you are Moses. I thought you'd run off on me."

"No sir, I wouldn't do that." Moses said truthfully. He hadn't run off….yet.

"Where's Jane, Samuel?" Mr. Kramer asked. "got to keep and eye on my property you know."

"She's right over there helping Rachel with the wash." Father reassured the man. Father was concerned. Why was Kramer so worried this time? He'd never lurked around so much before.

"What's with you Kramer? Are you afraid they're going to run away?"

"No. Just keeping my eyes and ears open, Samuel." Kramer left after that and hadn't been back in two days.

They would hide Moses and Jane in the attic until tomorrow night. Then they would get into the secret compartment in the wagon. Ben didn't know the secret yet because Father wasn't sure that he could trust him.

Later that evening after supper, Father and Mother gathered the children in the kitchen. It was time to tell everyone the secret. Joseph sat very still and twisted his hands.

"'Boys, Moses and Jane are hiding in the attic. You must not say anything about them to anyone or they will be caught and I will be in serious trouble. They are going with us to Indiana. They will be hiding in a secret place in the wagon." Father looked at the children with a solemn face. "Do you have any questions?"

The boy looked at one another. Six pairs of blue eyes stared back at Father. Joseph looked at his hands.

"Father," James asked, "Can we take Gran's pies with us?" Father looked startled for moment and then he laughed. He picked up the little boy and held him in his strong arms. "As many as we can fit into the wagon, James my pieboy." The rest of the children laughed and baby Mary gurgled and smiled in Mother's arms. It was time for prayers and bedtime. The boys gave their parents a goodnight hug and kiss .

Joseph was the last to leave. A new idea had just come to him. "I don't want to leave Virginia, Father. I was wondering if I could stay with Grandmother Bly for awhile. I will help her and maybe later on I can join you." Many years later, he thought.

"Joseph, how can you think of that?" Mother asked in a hurt voice. "I would miss you and could not think of going to Indiana without you."

"Joseph," Father asked, "did you hint to Mr. Kramer that Moses and Jane were going with us?"

"No, I didn't Father. I thought about it, but I wouldn't want to get you or Moses into trouble. Besides, I don't like Mr. Kramer. He's mean to everyone."

"I didn't think you would, Joseph. I'll make you a bargain. If you start with us on the journey and stay for two months, at the end of that time I'll send you to Grandmother's if you 're still not happy. How's that?" Father said as he put his hand to seal the bargain.

"It's a deal." Joseph said uncertainly as he shook his father's hand. He went up the stairs shaking his head and muttering to himself.

"We have raised some strong children Rachel." Father said to Mother as they went to bed.

"Yes, Samuel, they're just like their father, but I am worried about Joseph." Mother said.

"Don't trouble yourself dear. Once we get on the road he'll be fine."

Joseph couldn't sleep. He wanted to tell John how he felt, but he didn't know how to begin. He shook John's shoulder and said the first thing that came to his mind.

"John," Joseph whispered.

"Hmm?" John asked sleepily.

"Why do we call our parents Father and Mother instead of Pa and Ma like others do?" He tried to make the question seem very important.

John turned over and glared at his brother. "Joseph , you ask the dumbest questions sometimes. It's because Mother called her parents that. It shows respect or somethin' . That' s why they call us by our whole names, too. Respect for us I guess ...geez go ta' sleep will ya?" John rolled over and was asleep in seconds.

Joseph lay awake. Oh bother, he thought, I hope he doesn't remember that dumb question tomorrow. To cheer himself up Joseph began thinking about how it would be when he came back home to Gran's house. A smile was on his face when he fell asleep.

CHAPTER THREE

Journey Begins

It was June 1, 1850. Mother woke the boys up before dawn. "It's time to get up children. This is the big day. Father is already up and he wants you to help him right now."

The boys eagerly put their clothes on and went downstairs to the kitchen. All except for Joseph. He took as long as possible and slowly went down the stairs. Mother served them grits and potatoes with some pork sausage. They drank buttermilk and then hurried outside to help. The front yard was a mass of activity. Father and Ben were loading the last of the furniture and bedding onto the wagon. Grandmother Bly was checking over the harnesses. Uncle Zeke Harding was tying the canvas top down tightly, and assorted cousins and other relatives were loading foodstuffs onto the wagon.

"John, you go gather the last of the eggs for your mother and get those hens into the crates. James, you help John. David and Isaac you go get the horses and make sure their hooves are clean and their coats are burr free. I don't want them to get sores from the harnesses. Jock and Dobbin have to take us a long way and we need to give them special care. The rest of you help out where you can. I want to get on the way shortly." Everyone scattered. Father meant business. Anyone not doing his fair share would be punished. Besides, they were as eager as Father to get on the trail.

No one noticed Joseph hanging around Jock and Dobbin. He seemed to be talking to the big farm horses. He had tears in eyes. With everyone doing his part, the family was loaded and ready to go as the sun peeked over the hills. Mother and Grandmother Bly were openly crying as they hugged and kissed each other goodbye. Father hurried Mother onto the wagon. All of the boys had a lump in their throats as they said goodbye to the white house on the hill. It was the only home that they had ever known and Indiana seemed scary and far away to them. Father saw the sad faces around him and smiled.

"It's going to be fine. Everyone now, say goodbye to the old and hello to the new. I want to see smiles on all of these sad faces." Everyone, including Mother tried to smile. Although the smiles were a little lopsided they all felt better. All of a sudden, baby Mary started crying. Before the rest could join her, Father started singing a rousing hymn in his deep, baritone voice. Everyone joined him and drowned out Mary's howls. Father flicked the reins, and Jock and Dobbin began to move out of the yard. The horses started off down the lane but the wagon stood still! The reins were pulled right out of Father's hands. Everyone looked speechless as the horses trotted down the lane without the wagon or the family.

Father looked around. Only Joseph did not look surprised. The culprit was obvious.

"Joseph!" Father roared. "WHAT IS THE MEANING OF THIS! Go get those horses now before I put you in the harness!" Father's face was beet red and he was clenching and unclenching his hands. Joseph had never in his whole life seen his father so angry. Joseph ran down the lane faster than he had ever run in his life. He caught the big dray horses just as they reached the main road. He started back as quickly as he could get the two giant horses to move.

"Move faster boy before I come down from this wagon to help you!" Father bellowed from the wagon seat.

"Yes sir!" Joseph called breathlessly as he hurried back to the wagon.

Grandmother Bly couldn't help herself. After the initial shock of seeing the horses take off, she began to smile, then she chuckled and finally, she broke out in laughter. She had never seen anything like it. She had never seen Samuel so upset. The startled looks on everyone's faces was so funny that a body couldn't help but laugh. When Grandmother Bly started to laugh it began a chain of laughter that once started was hard to stop. Even Father had the beginning of a smile on his face and he wasn't as red as he had been. When Joseph returned with the horses Father got down off of the wagon seat and grabbed the horses reins out of Joseph's hands.

"You get in the back of the wagon Joseph. I'll deal with you later." Father re-hitched the horses to the wagon and checked each of the harnesses. Then he walked to the edge of the yard and took a branch off of a willow tree.

"For Later." He told Mother grimly. Again he flicked the reins over the horses heads and called "Gee Haw!" This time the wagon and horses went down the lane together. The Hardings were on their way to their new home.

The boys got off of the wagon and walked beside it for most of the morning. David and Isaac walked with the extra horses. All except for Joseph. He sat in the back of the wagon and waited nervously for his punishment.

It was a beautiful summer day. The sun was shining, there was a slight breeze, and the sky was a robin's egg blue. The road was dusty and the boys' feet were white by the time Father called a halt for lunch. He had pulled up near a stream. Mother got the lunch basket out. Then she went under the wagon and tapped two times, waited and tapped two more times. In a minute, Moses and Jane crawled out of the secret chamber under the wagon.

Ben rode up just as Moses helped Jane out of the wagon bed. He looked surprised, but not upset. He just smiled and began to do his assigned chores.

"Ben, I need to talk with you for a moment. Will you please walk with me for a minute?" Ben nodded and so he and Father walked over to a tall, oak tree. They talked for a few minutes and came back to the camp. Ben walked up to Moses, shook his hand, and smiled without saying a word. Then, he went to finish his chores. Father smiled broadly and shared a silent message with Mother.

Then Father called, "Joseph, get out of the wagon. You and I have some business to attend to."

Joseph came out of the wagon. He and Father walked behind some bushes.

"I don't want to do this son, but what you did today was dangerous. It didn't keep us from leaving did it?"

"No Sir." Joseph's lip trembled, but he didn't want Father to see that he was scared. Father sighed. "Bend over, son." Joseph bent over and Father gave him three strikes across the legs with the switch. It hurt like the devil.

"Get back into the wagon. You won't be eating with us." Father told Joseph. "I want no more pranks. Is that clear?"

"Yes sir." Joseph said tearfully.

Moses and Jane walked around stretching their arms and legs.

"Is it safe here, Missus?" Moses asked. "I sure would like to stretch my legs, and Jane is feeling mighty uncomfortable, but we don't want to get caught."

"I think you'll be safe here under these trees Moses." Mother assured them. "You can eat and stretch your legs for a few minutes while we have the noon meal. If someone comes, you hide in those bushes behind you until they leave."

"Rachel," Father called to Mother, "I don't think they should be out until dark." Father stated. "At least not until we get out of Virginia. It's too dangerous."

"Samuel, it's too cramped in that wagon for them to ride for a whole day. I refuse to see them suffer in there. Besides, Jane cannot lay like that in her condition." Mother rarely spoke up to Father so the children watched in surprise as their father agreed.

"I suppose you're right but they'll have to stay hidden."

"Yes sir." said Moses. "We'll stay here in these woods till it's time to load up again."

Mother and Father served the picnic meal. David and Isaac fed and watered the horses. The other children rested for the long walk to come. Baby Mary slept in her cradle while James fanned the air above her to keep the flies away.

As soon as dinner was over they were on their way again. They traveled seven miles that first day. Everyone was tired, but they knew it was only because it was the first day. The younger boys helped Mother cook the supper over the fire. Warren went to get firewood. Jane peeled potatoes under the wagon to keep out of sight.

Moses, Ben, and the older boys tended to the horses and checked the wagon for any repairs that needed to be done. After supper, Father sang some hymns, said the evening prayers and told everyone to get to sleep. There were no arguments. Everyone was tired, even Joseph.

CHAPTER FOUR

The Big Scare

The family was up and on the road before first light the next day. Everyone was anxious to be on the way. Everyone, that is, but Joseph. He was the last one to get up and the last one to start moving. When they had good roads that were dry and rut free the travelers made fifteen to twenty miles a day. When it was rainy or when the road was full of ruts, they made only ten miles. Joseph was impatient when it rained. The horses had to slow to a laborious crawl. Everyone had to get out and walk beside the wagon to keep it free from mud. Joseph's job was to walk in front of the horses and move any rocks or stones that were hidden in the mud out of the horses way. He hated it. If he wasn't fast enough, David fussed at him for being too slow. If he didn't walk far enough ahead he risked being stepped on by one of the big horses' hooves.

"I don't know why someone else can't do this. Everyone else has an easier job than me. Even James can sit up in the wagon and watch Mary while Mother helps Father. It just isn't fair." Joseph grumbled as he sloshed down the road.

"What's the matter little brother?" Isaac asked as he rode by on Father's riding horse, Belle. "Look ahead Joseph. It's clearing up. The sun ought to come out soon. We'll probably camp soon. There's a clearing up ahead about a mile."

"Isaac, can I ride on Belle with you?" Joseph asked. "I'll look for rocks while I'm riding."

"All right. Since you've done such a good job I guess Father won't mind." Isaac lifted Joseph onto the horse. Joseph rode proudly in front of Isaac. This felt so much better than walking in the mud. Isaac was his favorite brother. He was kind to Joseph and the other younger children. He didn't fuss as much as David did. Isaac and Joseph looked the most alike too. Their hair was a rich, dark brown with a hint of curl to it. Their eyes were clear lake blue with a dark rim around the iris. They already had laugh lines around their eyes from laughing so much. Isaac's body was that of a man. He was muscular and had a deep tan from working in the fields. He was taller than his father and older brother. Joseph had the body of a young boy about to change to a man although he was short for his age. He was skinny, and seemed to be all arms and legs. He, too, was tanned from working in the fields with his father and older brothers. He only went to school for three months a year. The rest of the time was spent in the fields planting, weeding, and harvesting the crops.

When Isaac and Joseph reached the clearing they began to gather wood for the evening fire. They had the fire going strong when the rest of the family go to the campsite.

"Looks like you have a good helper, Isaac." Mother said. "I wonder if I can borrow him to go fetch some water from the creek."

"I'll go Mother. Have Moses and Jane gotten out yet?" Joseph worried about the fugitives. He didn't think that he could have ridden cramped up like that for long.

"Yes, Father got them out a mile back so that they could stretch their legs a bit. It's so isolated out here that Father felt no one would see them. There they are now."

"How are you both doing ?" Mother asked the weary looking pair ."Why don't you go freshen up at the creek? Then Jane can help me with supper and Moses can help Samuel with that wheel that seems to be going bad."

Jane and Moses gave Mother a wan smile and walked off to the creek. Joseph followed the pair with the bucket. When they got to the creek, Jane and Moses knelt down and rinsed their faces off and took a long drink. Joseph filled the bucket and started back to camp. He turned around.

"How do you stand it?" I mean, how can you stand being cramped up in that wagon bed all day long? I don't think I could do it." Joseph's words spilled out of his mouth. He had been thinking about this for awhile.

"Joseph," Moses said. "Jane and me are the only family each of us has left. My mama was sold to a man in Georgia when I was younger than you. My daddy died before I was born. Jane's family is dead or gone to other masters. Jane and I can't bear the idea of being sold separately. We want to be free, Joseph. Do you know what that means? You don't I guess 'cause you have always been free. Imagine yourself like those horses drawing the wagon. They have to do what your father says or they might get beaten, or starved, or sold off to someone else. That's what Jane and me are, Joseph, livestock. We want to live like human beings because that's what we are. Our fathers were free men in Africa. Do you understand now why we would do anything to get to freedom? Your parents are good people and Jane and me is thankful for them." Moses finished and looked at Joseph seriously.

"Joseph," Jane said softly. "Moses and I are going to have a baby. We don't want him to be a slave. We want him to be a free man."

"Oh," said Joseph. "I think I understand. But tell me what you do all day. I mean, I'd go crazy not doing anything and not moving. You must be bored to death."

Moses laughed. "We dream Joseph. We talk about what our life will be like. We share little jokes, and we pray. Now come'n Joseph. Your mama is waiting for that water and we all has chores to do."

The threesome returned to the camp. Father and the boys were working on the wagon wheel. One of the spokes was loose and the rim was tearing off. Moses hurried over and lifted the wheel off the ground. He was a very big man. He seemed strong enough to lift the entire wagon.

Jane , however, was tiny and delicate looking. She seemed frail compared to Moses. But she was strong in her way. She helped Mother lift the cooking pot and then she tended to baby Mary who was fussing with hunger. Mother called everyone to supper. After supper, Joseph and James helped Mother clear up the cooking area. Father sat on a camp chair near the fire and read from the Bible. He was just beginning to read when the sound of hoofbeats came into the camp.

"Quickly, Moses! You and Jane hide in that clump of bushes over there." Father pointed to a dark area of brush about one hundred feet from the campsite. Moses lifted Jane and ran into the bushes. They faded into the darkness and the rest of the family turned to Father who began reading the Bible again.

A horse came galloping around the bend and the rider pulled the horse to a stop when he saw the campfire. The horse and rider both looked exhausted and the man almost fell off the horse when he dismounted.

"Please, could I bother you for a drink of water for my horse and me? We've been going hard for nigh on to an hour and my horse is about to drop. He's not young and isn't used to running this hard. Oh, please forgive me. My name is Adams Jones. My manners aren't usually this poor, but I'm terribly worried. My wife is having a baby and I'm riding into town to get the doctor." The young man ran a hand through his hair as he gulped down the water that Joseph handed to him.

Father pulled the man over to the fire and handed him a cup of coffee. "Where is your home Adam?" Father asked. "Perhaps my wife can be of some help until you come back with the doctor."

Adam looked as if he might cry. "Oh would you, Ma'am? I'd be so grateful. Ellen, that's my wife, is so frightened of being alone. We just came out here from Boston last year and she left all of her family behind. The farm is about ten miles down the road. Look for a pond on the left and a road by it. The house is on the other side of the pond. I need to be going on for the doctor." Adam jumped onto the horse's back as he gave the directions to the house. "Thank you!" He yelled as he galloped quickly down the road.

Mother gathered her things together and got up on Isaac's horse. Father got up on the horse behind her.

"Take care of everyone David." Father instructed as he and mother cantered to the farm. "You can finish that Bible passage and say the evening prayers. Oh, and don't forget Moses and Jane." He called as they disappeared into the darkness.

David finished reading the verse from Psalms and led the family in the evening prayers. They added an extra prayer for Adam and Ellen tonight. Moses helped David settle everyone for bed, and Jane held Mary until she fell asleep. Joseph fell asleep hoping that Father and Mother would return soon and that Ellen's baby would be fine.

"Wake up everyone, wake up. Rise and shine you sleepyheads." Mother called out. Joseph opened sleep-filled eyes just a slit and saw that the sun was shining brightly, and Mother was spooning batter onto the griddle. "What about the baby?" asked Joseph rubbing his gritty eyes.

"The Jones' have a beautiful baby girl." Father told everyone as he brought an armful of firewood to Mother. Mother and Jane finished fixing breakfast. They were all stuffed with as many hotcakes as they could hold. After breakfast, the family loaded up the wagon and Moses and Jane got back into their hiding place. The horses were hitched up and Father gave the signal. The wagon began to roll down the road. Later, they passed the pond where Ellen and her family lived. Father pulled the horses into the lane and they were soon at the house. Mother went to the house and knocked. Adam opened the door with a big grin on his face.

"I'm so glad you've come. Ellen was just asking me if you were going to stop when you came this way. We want you to come in and see the baby. Without your help Ellen and the baby might not have made it."

Father nodded and everyone got down off the wagon or off their horses. Moses and Jane, however, stayed where they were. Father didn't want to take any chances since they were still in a slave state.

The baby sure is tiny, Joseph thought, but he didn't say anything.

Ellen had named her baby Rachel after Mother. They stayed a short time and then after a look was exchanged between Mother and Father they bid good bye to the young couple and loaded all of the children onto the wagon and horses. They were off again towards Indiana.

The wagon had gone about three miles along a very dusty road when Joseph asked Mother if he could get down and walk in front for awhile.

"Just stay in front and don't lag behind. Take your brothers with you." James, John, William, and Warren jumped off of the wagon with Joseph. The boys skipped rocks for awhile and then they played tag until they were winded. John was just about to ask Mother for some water when he and the others heard rapid hoofbeats approaching. The children scattered to the side of the road as a group of horses galloped up to the wagon. The horses were dusty and so were the men riding them. There were five men and they all had guns and holsters. Rolled whips were wrapped around each of their saddle horns. Joseph thought that they looked awfully mean and fierce. They were all bearded and had handkerchiefs around their necks.

"Have ya' seen a Nigra couple on this here road?" one of the men asked Father.

"No. I haven't. We haven't seen anyone on this road for two days." Father answered .

The men shifted in their saddles. The man who seemed to be the leader stared hard at Father. "Then you won't mind if we search yer wagon will ya mister?" As he spoke, he and the other men drew their guns and pointed them at Father, Mother, and Ben. David made a move toward Mother and the leader fired above David's head. Mother let out a small scream.

"Now folks, don't worry. Me and the boys are just doing a job. As soon as we check out the wagon we'll be on our way. All right boys you know what to do. Be sure and check the flooring of the wagon good. One old guy near Wheeling had a false bottom in his wagon. He was hiding them Nigras in it. We got him and the runaways." The leader said. He kept his gun pointed at Father's head as the other men started toward the wagon.

Joseph felt something or someone make him approach the leader. He looked up in terror at the man. "Mister," he asked in a quavering voice, "are you a slave catcher?'

"Sure am sonny. Ya' know sometin' about these runaways?"

"Well, do I get a reward if I tell you?" Joseph asked. The words seemed to be coming out of his mouth as though a voice was telling him what to say. His knees were knocking together, and he couldn't have spit if he had to as he stood there looking up at the grizzly man.

"Of course, boy, we'll share the reward with you. " The man said and then he laughed.

"I saw the two nigras about five miles back. They ran across the road after we went by. I was looking for a marble I'd lost and that's when I saw them. They was looking real scared and the lady got her shawl caught in the bushes. The man got it loose and they ran into the woods heading north." Joseph looked up at the man. He was amazed at what had just come out of his mouth. He looked up at the man blankly. His brothers looked at him as though he had just sprouted horns, tails, and a mule's ears.

The leader leaned down and looked in Joseph's eyes. Joseph stared innocently back at him. "Boy, you're going to show me where this tree is. Maybe there's some other tracks there too."

"No!" You can't take him. He's just a boy!" Mother and Father protested ,but the leader ignored them. He and Joseph rode off down the road. The leader left the other four men to guard the rest of the family. The children sat huddled in the road watching the men in fear and anger.

Now what have I done? Joseph thought fearfully as he and bounty hunter galloped down the road. What if he doesn't believe me? What if they decided to search the wagon anyway? Joseph felt like he was going to throw up.

"Mister," Joseph called, "I think I'm going to be sick."

"You do and I'll shoot you, boy." The man growled. Joseph clenched his arms around the man's waist and had a serious talk with his stomach.

Meanwhile, the other children sat huddled in the road. Time seemed to stop. John had rung his shirt tail into a rag. Mary howled loudly and the other slave catchers were beginning to look impatient. They were swinging their guns around at the children. Finally, the leader came around the curve in the road with Joseph clutching his waist.

"The boy was right. Found the bushes with the pieces of cloth on it. I also saw the set of tracks heading north in the woods just like he said."

The man flung a pale Joseph off of his horse. "They must be backtracking towards the east. Let's go boys. Sorry for the delay folks, but we're just doing our job."

"What about my money?" Joseph called in a quivery voice to the man as they began riding back down the road. He really didn't want it, but again the voice made him say it.

"Sorry, sonny. You don't get paid unless you catch the runaways. Since you helped us out we won't kill your family." The man said and then shot a few rounds into the air above Joseph's head as he galloped away.

Joseph angrily shook his fist at the man as he rode away. Then, as soon as the men were out of sight, he turned toward his family, smiled faintly and promptly threw up.

"Oh Joseph," his mother said as she jumped off of the wagon, wiped his face, and gave him a big hug. "You frightened me to death. But I am so proud of you. How did you ever think of that story?"

"Son, you saved the day. That was some quick thinking." Father said as he ruffled his hair.

"Joseph, how DID you think of that story?" Mother repeated impatiently.

"Well," said Joseph, "Remember Mother did hook her robe on a bush when we camped last night. So, I just took them there. I showed him the woods where we all took a nature break. It had our footprints. He believed that's where they were headed. I knew Father would think of something but I thought maybe the leader would believe a boy more than a man. I guess I just got lucky or maybe we just got lucky. I was so afraid that if they started looking in the wagon that they would find the false bottom. Then, we'd all be in trouble."

John gave Joseph a big hug and so did his other brothers. There was no need for words. Joseph was the hero of the day and everyone was grateful for him. The family traveled a few more miles that afternoon and then they stopped for the night. Mother made a cake to celebrated Joseph's bravery.

Moses and Jane couldn't stop thanking Joseph until finally he blushed a bright red and begged them to stop.

Father said a special prayer that night. "We thank thee, Father for the bravery of our boy, Joseph. We thank thee for keeping him safe. Lord, keep us safe in your hands for the rest of our journey. We praise thee Lord. Amen."

CHAPTER FIVE

Along The Ohio River

The family loaded up the wagon later than usual the next morning. With all of the excitement the night before, Mother and Father decided that everyone needed a longer rest before heading out. Joseph was still the hero for the day and Mother let him ride in the wagon. Joseph was very uncomfortable with all of the attention and before long he asked Mother if he could get down and walk with the other boys.

"Certainly, son. I just thought that you might like to ride with me for awhile. You had a big day yesterday and Father and I felt you needed some time for yourself. " Mother was patting Mary on the back trying to get a gas bubble out of her. Mary had been cranky all morning.

"No ma'am. I'd rather be with James and John if you don't mind." Mother nodded yes as she continued to rub Mary's back.

Joseph hopped down off of the wagon and joined his brothers. "Hey John, wanna pitch stones?" he asked his older brother.

"Sure." John picked up a stone and began the game. The boys played different games throughout the day making the time pass quickly. All too soon Mother told them to begin gathering firewood as dusk was upon them.

"Put the wood up there by that stream." Mother pointed to a stream about a half a mile up the road. The boys gathered armloads of wood and brought it to the stream. Father and the older boys had started to make camp. Mother came up with the wagon and everyone began their evening tasks. Moses and Jane came out of their hiding place, but they stayed in the shadows. Nobody wanted to take any chances. After dinner, Father announced that they would pick up the pace beginning tomorrow.

"We're falling behind our schedule. We won't get to Indiana before winter if we don't travel more miles everyday. We'll start earlier and travel until dusk. I want to get to Parkersburg within a week if possible. Then, we'll follow the Ohio River all the way to Indiana. It might not be as quick as going overland but I know we won't get lost and the chances of being bothered by slave catchers might be less than if we go through Ohio on the National Road."

"But Father," David said. "Wouldn't Ohio be safer than going through Kentucky? Kentucky is a slave state. Ohio is a free state. Won't Moses and Jane be safe if we cross over into Ohio? The slave catchers can't take them in a free state can they?

"I'm sorry to say they can take them David. If they can show proof of ownership and an accurate description, they can take them back to their masters. I have heard that Ohio is full of bounty hunters trying to make it rich by catching unsuspecting slaves running north. We have to get Moses and Jane far away from here and change their identities. It may mean that they will have to go to Michigan or even Canada to ensure their freedom."

Father paced back and forth as he talked. Then he stopped and turned to face his family and friends.

"Enough of this. Let's say our prayers and turn in for the night. We'll worry about the next leg of our journey when we reach Parkersburg." As Father prayed, Joseph looked around at his family, Ben, Moses , and Jane. He felt safe, secure, and scared at the same time. He wanted to run back down the road to his old home. He looked at his brothers. They seemed to mirror his feelings in their eyes. Warren grinned at him. John nodded. James reached for his hand and the older brothers made a thumbs up signal. The next morning got off to a bad start. Bad luck continued throughout the day. It was raining so Mother couldn't start a fire. Everyone choked down cold, hard biscuits and washed them down with water. Even Father was grumpy without his morning coffee. Mary cried from the moment she woke up and didn't stop. They plodded through the rain. It was slow going because the wheels were mired down in mud. The horses strained against their harnesses and were tired out early in the day. Their heads hung low and they made disgruntled whinnying sounds. Joseph stayed in the wagon as long as he could, but Mary's crying was about to make him scream. He decided the rain and mud were better than listening to Mary.

"Ya wanna get down and look for tadpoles?" he asked James who was sitting with his hands over his ears in misery.

"Sure. Let's go." James said. He was out of the wagon before the words were out of his mouth.

"Boys, don't stray far and put on your raingear." Mother called to them. They threw their cloth ponchos over their heads and started tracking down puddles of water.

About an hour later they hadn't found one tadpole and they were getting discouraged. Startled by rustling sound coming from the woods, they both froze. Father had warned them about wild boars and other animals that might be foraging in the forests around them. The wagon was about a fourth of a mile ahead but they didn't want to yell for fear of calling attention t themselves.

"What should we do Joseph? I'm scared." James huddled behind Joseph, his lips quivering.

"Me too. Let's just head toward the wagon as quietly as possible. Maybe that beast won't hear us." As the boys began to tiptoe down the road toward the wagon, the rustling noise got louder now mixed with a whining and shuffling. Both boys were picking up speed and began hot footing it down the road when something burst out the woods and gave chase. Neither Joseph or James looked back. They broke into a run. The beast was closing in. Joseph could feel its hot breath on his back. Heavy panting echoed in his ears. James had run so fast that he was ahead of Joseph. Joseph tried to run faster but the monster kept pace. All of a sudden - thump - the beast pushed Joseph to the ground and began to sniff and lick Joseph's ears. Lick his ears? Joseph thought maybe the beast was getting him ready for his next meal. Then he heard laughter. He looked up and James was doubled over gasping with glee. Joseph rolled over and looked up into the face of the ugliest hound dog with the longest ears he'd ever seen. The dog was grinning at him and began to bark in a joyous way.

"What the heck!" Joseph sputtered. The dog jumped around him planting a slurpy tongue here and there. James grabbed the dog around the neck so Joseph could get up. When Joseph stood up he took a look at the hound. The dog gave a playful bark and got out of James's grasp. Then he ran toward the wagon. He turned once and looked back at the boys as if to say, "You guys coming? Hurry Up!" Joseph looked up at his brother and they both began laughing. They ran to catch up with their new friend.

"Mother, look who found us." Joseph panted as he caught up to the dog and the wagon. Mary was still crying and Mother looked very frazzled. When she saw the hound at the boys' feet she sniffed.

"That's exactly what we don't need boys. A dog is just another burden right now. I have enough problems without worrying about a hound." Mother said. Father rode up.

"What have we here, boys? That's a fine looking pup. About six months old I wager." Father patted the dog's head and felt its ears and back. "This animal's in good shape. It's been well taken care of. Probably belongs to someone nearby. We'll hold on to it in case they come looking for it."

"Can't we keep him Father?" Joseph asked longingly. He was already forming a bond with their beast from the forest.

"Not if the owner comes Joseph. That wouldn't be right. It would be stealing. This dog has been loved, you can tell by looking at him."

"But Father," Joseph said, "why can we keep Moses and Jane and not this dog? It's the same thing. Moses and Jane belong to someone too."

"I know it's hard to understand son, but this animal needs a master to take care of him. He needs food ,water and a place to sleep. He can't do that very well by himself.

Moses and Jane are people just like you and me. They have the right to take care of themselves. No one should own another person Joseph. It's not right."

Joseph tried to understand what Father was saying, but it was confusing.

Almost at the same time everyone looked toward the wagon. Mary had stopped crying. She was gurgling and cooing as she looked at the dog. The hound was standing on it's hind legs whining back at her. It was as if they were both talking together in their own language. Then, the clouds seem to float away and the sun broke through.

Father looked at Mother. She was looking at the hound with a bemused expression.

"Well, I believe this fellow is suppose to be here with us. What are you boys going to call him?"

"Traveler," said Joseph, "cause he's a traveler like us."

"Beast," said James, "that's what we thought he was out there."

"How about T.B. for short?" Father compromised. The boys agreed, so T.B. joined the family without further ceremony.

The family continued traveling toward Parkersburg with T.B. sniffing the trail ahead. He broke into a horrible howling the first night when Moses and Jane came out of their hiding place. He sniffed each of them up and down and then bayed at them until Father got him under control with a birch switch. He wasn't cruel to T.B. he just tapped him with the switch until he stopped howling. Then, he gave him a pat on the head and said "Good dog."T. B. soon got the idea and gave Moses and Jane each a slurp of his wet tongue. He lay down at their feet. Moses and Jane laughed nervously.

"Why did T.B. do that Father?" John asked. Joseph had a good idea what Father's answer would be. Memories of the slave drivers came back to him. Joseph felt that T.B. was probably a slave catching dog. Wasn't it wonderful that Joseph had found him so that he could be a good dog from now on?

The family pushed on to Parkersburg eagerly. They were all anxious to see a town once again, especially other people. After what seemed like years, but was only a few weeks, they pulled into Parkersburg. The children were amazed.

Parkersburg was a big city compared to the small towns along the way. Wagons, carriages, horses, carts, and people crowded the streets. It seemed that everyone was going west just like Joseph and his family. Father cautioned everyone to stay close.

"If you wander off you might get lost in this crowd. We don't want to spend valuable time looking for you. We will have a hard time finding you. All of you younger children get in the wagon now. You older boys stay on your horses. I'm going to park us under that big oak tree over there. Then, I'm going to see about getting us down river."

Father guided the group over to the oak tree. As soon as he saw that everyone was settled, he went off to the river front.

Joseph, James, and John watched the crowds of people from the back of the wagon.

"Look at all those people! Where do you think they're going? I wonder if they're going to Indiana like we are?" Joseph asked. He didn't expect an answer from his brothers. They didn't know either.

An old man was sitting under the tree about ten feet from the wagon. His chin rested on his chest and he seemed to be sound asleep. He raised his head up and squinted at the boys leaning out of the wagon. He had heard Joseph's questions and called to the boys.

"Don't you boys know what's going on?" He asked. The boys shook their heads. "Why it's gold boys. There's gold in California. That's where all these folks is headed. Before the gold strike this town was as dead as two rusty nails. Now it's a boom town and a man can't get any sleep anywhere in this here place. I'm gonna hafta move along to get any peace."

The old man kept muttering to himself as he shuffled off down the lane behind the oak tree.

"Did you hear that Mother?" Joseph called. He scrambled through the wagon to reach his mother who was sitting on the front seat with Mary in her arms. "That old man says that there is gold in California. Where's California?"

"California is far west of here Joseph," Mother replied. "It's much farther west than Indiana. It would take months to get there. Thank goodness that's not where we're going."

Joseph looked at his older brothers who were sitting on their horses in front of the wagon. He knew they were acting as guards to protect the family from anyone who got to close. Isaac was talking to a man on foot who had a pack on his back.

"Yes sir, young man, you ought to go out to the goldfields. You could become a rich man in a matter of days. I hear that there are nuggets as big as your fist just lying in the dirt ready for the picking." Isaac said something to the man that Joseph couldn't understand. The man nodded and then moved on down the dusty road. He turned once and waved back.

"Mother," Joseph whispered. "What about Moses and Jane?" They must be awful miserable by now. When can we let them out?"

"I'm hoping when Father gets back we can put up a tent around this tree and let them out for a little while, son. But we have to be extra careful in town. Any one of these people could be looking for runaway slaves. This would be perfect place to find them. I am worried about Jane though. Her time is getting near and I know she's uncomfortable.

Look! Here comes your father now." Mother leaned forward towards Father as he approached the wagon.

"Have you heard?" Father asked.

"Do you mean about the gold, Father?" Joseph asked scooting over to make room.

"Exactly," Father said. "We need to get out of this town today. I would like to stay but the prices in the stores are completely unreasonable and the crowds are dangerous. We are going to travel down river on land instead of by boat. The captains on the boats are charging fifty dollars a wagon to go down to Huntington. We don't have that kind of money. It will take us longer but we have no other choice. Let's get everyone out of this town before something happens. There are too many gunslingers and 'no goods' in this place just looking for trouble."

Father turned his horse around and Mother released the brake on the wagon.

"Gee Haw!" she called as she gathered the reins in her hands and guided the horses down the crowded, congested street. They followed Father down the main street of town and out into the countryside down a well worn road. The younger boys got out and walked ahead of the wagon. They stayed by the side of the road because wagon traffic, horseback riders, and people on foot had created a packed, busy roadway and they didn't want to get separated.

"I've never seen so many people in my entire born days." Joseph exclaimed as he stared at the crowds of all kinds of people. "Have you John?"

"No! I thought I'd seen a lot at the county fair back home, but that was nothing compared to this. Where could all these people be coming from? I wonder why they're leaving their homes to go west. They can't ALL have gold fever." John said thoughtfully.

"Maybe they're criminals like murderers and they're running away from the law." Joseph said. Then he thought about Moses and Jane. We're criminals too! Oh why wasn't he back home under his old elm tree?

To take his mind off those thoughts, Joseph looked at a scruffy, angry looking man with a drooping mustache who was passing them on a lean horse.

"Look at him. He looks like he coulda' just robbed a bank." Joseph told the others.

James looked fearfully at the man and ran back to the wagon.

"Now look what you've done. He's scared to death." John admonished his brother.

Joseph ran after James who was climbing into the wagon.

"I didn't mean to scare you, Jamey. He did look mean though' didn't he?" As James nodded tearfully, a loud thumping sound came from the floor of the wagon. The sound increased in volume and sounded frantic.

Joseph and James bent down and put their ears close to the wagon bottom..

"Moses?" Joseph called.

"Help us!" A frantic voice rasped from the floorboards.

"Moses, we're just leaving Parkersburg. I'll tell Mother that you need help." Joseph said as he scrambled toward the front of the wagon.

"Mother! Moses is calling for help. He was beating on the wagon floor. James and I heard him. He wants our help Mother. What should we do?"

"We'll pull over into that grove of trees there and see what the problem is." Mother said as she pointed to a grove of trees about twenty feet off of the main road. She pulled on the reins and guided the team towards the trees.

Joseph ran to the back of the wagon and yelled to the floor. "We're pulling over. Moses hang on!"

Father rode up and asked "What's wrong?" Mother explained the problem as she got down off the wagon seat. Father was already undoing the secret panel and helping Moses and Jane out of the hiding place before Mother finished.

Jane was doubled over in pain clutching her abdomen.

"Well, it's quite obvious what the problem is," Mother said. "Jane's baby is coming. We'll be stopping here Samuel. You and the boys need to set up the tent and make sure that we have no unexpected company. Joseph, you and William watch Mary and James. John, you go get firewood with Warren. Jane, honey, you come with me.

Moses you can help with the tent, but stay in the trees. Now, does everyone know what to do?" Mother didn't expect any answers as she put a kerchief around her golden, brown hair and put a fresh apron on and tied it around her tiny waist. She put her right arm around Jane's shoulders and held her hand with her left hand. Her right hand motioned towards everyone to get busy with their assigned tasks.

Father, Moses, Ben, and the older boys got the tent up in record time. Then, they built a makeshift corral in front of the tent and put the horses inside it. If anyone approached their campsite the horses would whinny and alert them. T.B. seemed to understand what was gong on because he sat in front of the horses looking out onto the road. He was on guard duty.

Mother and Jane went inside the tent. Father had set up a cot for Jane and moved a small table from the wagon to the tent for Mother to use. Jane laid down on the cot while

Mother got her supplies set up on the table. She called for Father to heat some water, bring her towels and her sewing box.

Jane was moaning and whimpering inside the tent, but she didn't scream. Screaming might bring unwanted, curious visitors. Mother came out of the tent briefly. She looked at the worried looks on everyone's faces.

"David, you and Isaac take everyone to the river for a wash and swim. Here is some food for a picnic dinner down there. Keep them there until Father comes for you or it gets to be nightfall. I don't need anyone underfoot right now, and there's no need for the little ones to worry."

"Yes Ma'am, " David said as he picked up the basket and herded his younger brothers toward the river.

"Come on boys, I'll race you," he challenged. Away they raced.

Joseph looked behind at the tent and worried about Jane. She'd be fine if we were still back home, he thought as he followed David. Even though she'd be at Mr. Kramer's Mother would still look after her.

Father held Mary while Moses paced back and forth under the trees. He was well hidden by the tent and the horses, but he was careful to stay in the trees' shadows just in case. Mary started to fuss after an hour. She began to cry and Mother came out of the tent.

"If you could only feed her." Mother teased Father.

"Moses, you go in and hold Jane's hand while I change Mary. Jane just needs some company right now." No sooner had Moses gone in the tent when Jane let out a muffled scream. Mother jerked her head up, thrust the baby into Father's arms and ran into the tent. Moses came running out of the tent as pale as a clean sheet.

"What's wrong?" Samuel asked his friend. Moses couldn't reply. He just sat down on the ground, his whole body shaking.

Jane emitted another bloodcurdling scream and then both men heard the sound of a wailing baby. Moses put his head in his hands and began to cry. Father patted him on the back to soothe him and congratulate him. Mary started to wail in unison with the newborn. Mother came out of the tent. She pulled loose strands of hair off of her face and tucked them neatly into a chignon at the nape of her neck. She carefully wiped her face with her apron and looked at Moses.

"Go see your new son, Moses." She said softly. "Jane is asleep. She had a rough time because the baby was big and came so fast. But she'll be fine in a couple of days."

Moses tiptoed very quietly into the tent. There he saw his son lying next to his sleeping wife. Carefully, so that he wouldn't awaken Jane, he lifted the baby and held him in his arms. He whispered to his son, "I name you Abraham, the son of Moses. May you go and help your people. May you lead them as you would have done in our homeland. This is your homeland now. May you never be held in bondage and may you always be proud of who and what you are." Moses kissed his son and brought him outside.

The children had just returned from the river and were waiting for a chance to see the baby.

"Can we see him?" they all asked at once. Moses bent down to show them his son. The children crowded around him gawking at the new member of their traveling party.

"Kinda small isn't he? Warren asked.

"He's awful pale." observed John. "He's not as dark as you and Jane."

"When can we play with him?" James asked hopefully. Everyone laughed

Abraham just stared at the children with bright unfocused eyes.

Mother fixed an early supper and retired to the wagon early. She was exhausted from the day's events. The others sat around the fire for a time. Moses told them stories of Africa. Father told them stories of when he moved to western Virginia when he was Joseph's age.

"Gee Father, you and I are alike aren't we? We both left our homes at the same age. Did you want to leave your home? I'll bet you hated it like I did. Didn't you want to go back to your old home?"

"Oh yes, Joseph I did hate to leave my friends and family like you. But, I realized that it was the best thing to do at the time just like you will someday. Besides, it was a great adventure. One day I'll tell you all about it. Now it's time for everyone to turn in. We want to get an early start in the morning."

Despite sleepy protests the children were asleep in a short time. T.B. sat guarding outside of the tent with the new baby inside. The dog seemed to sense who needed his guardianship the most.

CHAPTER SIX

Sickness

Mother and Father decided to move farther on down the river road the next day. The road was too crowded for Moses and Jane to be safe.

Mother put Jane in the wagon and set a screen in front of her bed and barrels in front of the screen. Moses continued to ride in the secret compartment. The baby seemed to know that there was danger. He didn't cry very much. William rode in the wagon to help Jane and keep his eyes posted on the road behind them. If he saw anyone following them, he was to alert Mother.

They traveled down the river road for five days. The crowds were thinning out, but there were still more people along the road than they had expected. Jane was making a rapid recovery and the baby seemed to be growing daily.

Mary was fascinated by Abraham and she would remain quiet for a long time just looking at him. Jane kept Mary during the day now since she and Abraham had hit it off so well.

On the evening of the fifth day, they were just about to pull off the road to settle down for the night when Ben came riding up to the wagon. He had gone a head to find a campsite.

"There's a wagon up ahead. The people in it are real sick. The man is just about gone. His wife said their three children died two days ago. She's tending her husband, but she's not well herself."

"I'll go have a look." Mother said. "Joseph, get my medicine basket." Mother gathered her things and rode off with Ben on Belle. The boys set up the camp and got the cookfire started. Mother returned. Her face was serious. Ben's face was pale. He looked scared.

"Samuel, the woman is very sick. I don't think either of them are going to make it, but I must go help. It's cholera." Everyone in the camp shuddered. Cholera was deadly. The disease had killed many in their little community two years before. Mother had gotten the disease and almost died. Grandmother Bly had miraculously nursed her back to life. No one wanted her to tend to someone who could make her or others sick.

"Rachel, have you forgotten that you almost died from cholera? Do you want to risk that again? Not to mention exposing your children to it. I forbid you to help them Rachel. I can't take a chance that you will get sick." Father said as he held Mother gently in his arms ,but his voice was very stern.

Mother looked up at Father with what everyone in the family called Mother's 'Mule Look.' She could be as stubborn as six mules on a rainy day if she felt bound to do something.

"You forbid me, Samuel?" She asked in a soft voice. "Do you really think that you could stop me from helping those people? What are you going to do? Try and tie me up. I'm helping them and that's the end of the discussion." Mother said as she turned away from Father and began to gather more supplies.

Father grabbed her arm and said angrily, "I WILL not let you kill yourself for strangers when your own family needs you!"

Mother wrenched herself out of Father's grasp and mounted Belle.

"Samuel, Grandmother Bly said that most likely I would never get cholera again. Those that have it and survive usually never get it again. I'll be careful. If we were sick and someone came along, wouldn't you hope that they would take care of us? Now, you boil all the water like we've been doing and give everyone an extra pinch of salt with their supper. I'll be fine. You needn't worry."

Father grabbed the pommel of the saddle.

"Rachel, I couldn't stand losing you. Please be careful. Remember, we need you too." Father grasped Mother's hand and squeezed it. Mother touched Father's face gently. Then, she rode away.

It was quiet when she left. Joseph felt a lump in his throat. He was scared for Mother. He remembered when she was sick. It was the worst time of their lives. He didn't want that to happen again. He wished that they had never left home. Then Mother wouldn't be risking her life for strangers. Why couldn't that family just take care of themselves?

"All right boys let's get supper ready and boil some water for drinking and washing up. Let Moses out, Ben. Jane would you please tend to Mary until Rachel gets back? Come on children. Your Mother would want you to do your chores now." Father said. He directed everyone with a false enthusiasm that fooled no one.

Mother came back late that evening. Joseph heard her call softly to Father.

"Samuel? Don't come near me. I'm going to take off my clothes. I want you to burn them. Then, bring me some water and soap. Bring my nightgown too, so that I can put it on after I wash."

"Did the woman live?"

"No." Mother replied. "I don't want to talk now, Samuel. I just want to get these clothes off before the sickness goes from me to you and the children." Mother stood behind a sheet and began to take her dress off.

Father took Mother's clothes and burned them. He brought her cooled boiled water and she washed her body with lye soap. Joseph could just see her head from where he was under the wagon. She was wincing from the sting of the soap. He also saw tears in eyes.

"Mother." Joseph whispered.

Mother looked up. "Joseph, why are you awake? Do you realize how late it is? Go back to sleep."

"I'm sorry Mother. I mean about the lady. Why does God do things like that to people?"

"God didn't do this Joseph. They caught cholera from something or someone, and they weren't strong enough to fight it." Mother said. She looked very sad and worried.

"Do you think we'll catch it Mother?" Joseph asked as he crawled out from under the wagon.

"I pray that we don't. I'm worried about Mary, Moses, and Jane. You boys were exposed when I had it and didn't get sick. I hope that we are lucky again."

"Joseph! Go back to sleep and let your Mother finish. She's tired and she needs her rest the same as you do." Father said as he handed Mother her nightgown and dressing robe. Mother finished dressing and came out from behind the sheet. Joseph did as he was told.

"It's all right Samuel. Joseph helped me take my mind off that poor woman and her family. We'll have to bury her and burn their wagon tomorrow. It's too dangerous to just leave them on the road. I'm going to brew everyone some willow bark tea for breakfast, just in case." Mother laid down on her bedroll, closed her eyes and slept.

Father sat up for a long time staring into the fire. Joseph lay awake worrying about Mother. They wouldn't have this problem if they had stayed on the farm. Cholera had already come to them. It wouldn't come again. The two months were almost up. He could hardly wait to go back home.

The next day was gloomy with dark clouds hovering overhead. Father and Ben were up before sunrise. They burned the wagon and buried the poor family. When they returned, Mother was serving breakfast with Jane's help.

"How are you this morning?" Father asked Mother.

"I'll be fine. Just a little tired." Mother answered. "Did you take care of the wagon? I tried to look for something that would tell us their name, but I couldn't find anything, not even a Bible. I hate to just leave them there with no one knowing where they are now. I would like to let there kin know what happened."

"I found something." Father said. He took a worn looking leather folder out of his shirt. "Look," he said as he pulled out a book. "It's a diary. Her name was Addie Hopkins Meyer. Her husband was Josiah Meyer. She started the diary years ago when she was a girl. She even wrote her mother's address at the end of the book. She must have had a feeling that she wouldn't get back home."

"That's good. Now I can write them and let her family know. I'll feel better knowing I helped her in some way even though I couldn't save her." Mother said and then she started to cry.

"You children go get the horses and gear ready. Some of you help Jane clean up. We need to get on the road and away from here." Father said. He held Mother in his arms. She quietly sobbed against his chest.

I think I'll start keeping a diary. Joseph thought to himself. Maybe it will help me think of a way to get back home. I'll ask Father for some paper later.

The wagon rolled on down the road. As they passed the burned out wagon and graves of the Meyer family the boys gave a solemn salute. Father tipped the brim of his hat and Mother blew a kiss. It was a lonely, sad sight that they were glad to leave behind.

After they had traveled about a mile down the road, the sun began peeking from behind the clouds. Before too long, the sky had cleared. It was a beautiful summer day.

Joseph enjoyed the beautiful day, but he couldn't help thinking about the family that they had left behind. That could have been his family. He wondered why anyone would want to risk being buried out here in the wilderness all by themselves.

Joseph got paper that evening from Father. He began to write:

> *Today was very pretty. Mother was sad. I am too. I want to go home. A family died of cholera.*

For the next few days everything went perfectly. They met very few people along the road so Father told Moses to ride in the wagon with Jane for a time. He eagerly agreed.

Five days after they left the cholera wagon they stopped to camp on a bluff by the river. Mother sent the youngest boys down to the river to get water and firewood for supper.

"You boys can stay there and swim for awhile. Watch out for the little ones, Joseph. Don't forget to bring my water and firewood back with you."

Joseph and his brothers ran down to the river in a rush.

"Yippee! Last one there is a stuffed polecat!" cried Joseph as he ran down the bluff pulling his clothes off as he went.

"I'm coming faster than you brother!" called John as he zoomed by Joseph.

"Me too. Me too!" yelled Warren, William and James as they ran on short, skinny legs to the river's edge.

"I won!" shouted Joseph as he jumped into the water with just his littles on. His shirt and trousers were part of a path of strewn clothing left by he and his brothers.

"You won 'cause I let you." John said as dove in beside his brother. He was watching as the little boys came racing to the water's edge.

"Ha!" said Joseph. "Come on in James! It's wonderful in here. The water feels great. It's cool and there aren't many rocks on the bottom."

"I'm scared Joseph," James cried. "it seems deep to me."

"Here. I'll hold you." Joseph went to get him while John held on to the hands of Warren and William.

"Hey this is fun!" James giggled as he paddled around Joseph. "Gotcha!" he called as he splashed Joseph and John.

"Look at us! Look at us!" Warren called. He had William on his shoulders. William was trying to stand on his brother's narrow shoulders.

"Ohhhh!" William cried as he fell off and into the water. He came up sputtering water out of his mouth.

"Now, aren't you glad we made this trip?" John asked Joseph. "Isn't this great? What an adventure we're having."

"We can swim and have fun like this back home." Joseph argued. "We wouldn't have to take water to Mother. We had a well right outside the kitchen door. And the firewood pile was kept up by David, not us. So there. I'm going home you know. Father promised. It's been six weeks. Only two more weeks and I can go home. And I AM going home." Joseph stated as he walked toward shore. John had ruined the day for him. He gathered his clothes and got dressed. Leaving his brothers playing at the edge of the river, Joseph gathered firewood and took it to Mother.

"Father!" Joseph called. "Father can I talk to you for a minute, please?" he walked over to where his father was mending one of the harnesses.

"What's on your mind, son?" Father asked as he puffed on a corn stalk pipe. The tobacco smoke curled up and around Joseph, filling the air with a pungent spicy odor.

"Father, two months is about over. I still want to go home. Will you let me go? Are you going to keep your promise?"

"Look in that pouch over there." Father pointed to a pouch hanging on the wagon brake. "Open it."

Joseph opened it. Inside were gold coins and paper money. "That's our money for going west. If you still want to go home when we reach Huntington, I'll use some of that money to buy you a stage ticket back home. You understand that we need you in Indiana to help us get started, but I will send you back if that's what you want."

"Yes sir. I understand." Joseph said. He felt a sense of selfish relief. His father would do as he had promised.

"I'm sorry." He said without truly meaning it.

"Nothing to be sorry about, son. If that's the way you feel then that's the way it is." Father got up and patted Joseph on the back. He and Joseph walked over to the cookfire. Mother had supper ready.

Joseph wrote in his diary:

Went swimming today. Father says I can still go home.
I can hardly wait.

The sun shone on yet another day. Mother sang as she flicked the reins over the horses' backs. Father sat next to her studying his maps.

"We're taking a little longer than I had hoped, Rachel. I had wanted to get to Ike's by September 1. I don't think we'll make it until the end of September now. I was hoping to get in a winter crop before the snow comes. It's not looking good for this winter. I just hope Ike can help us this year."

"Don't worry dear, I'm sure Ike will help us all that he can. Besides, we're making good time now. We'll be fine."

Joseph listened to his parents from the back of the wagon. Hmph. He thought grumpily, we'd be fine if we were still back home. Which is where I will soon be. He thought happily.

David and Isaac rode ahead with Ben to scout the river road. The road had begun to narrow and Father wanted to make sure that it didn't end. Moses rode in the back of the wagon with Jane who was mending shirts and tending the two babies. The younger boys walked along the side of the wagon.

Suddenly, Joseph watched with concern as James clutched his stomach and ran for the woods. He came out a few minutes later.

"Mama!" he shrieked. "Mama help me!" he cried. He fell to the ground in agony.

Joseph ran to his little brother and gathered him in his arms.

"What's wrong James?" He asked. James didn't hear him. He was burning up and had turned very pale. As Joseph held him, James cried out, grasped his stomach. He got up and tried to run to the bushes. He didn't make it.

Mother caught him as he began to fall. A desperate look came over her face as she picked him up in her arms. She carried him back to the wagon and gently placed him down on the road. She looked up at Father with tears in her eyes.

"It's cholera." She whispered tearfully. Then, she tried to gather her strength.

"Pull the wagon over to that grove of trees. We'll put the tent here on this side of the road. We have to isolate him from everyone else. Come on everyone. Let's get going. Your lives depend on doing what I say. Go!"

Mother directed everyone like a general at war. No one questioned her. No one disputed one of her orders. Water and food were boiled. James's clothes were burned and he was given huge amounts of boiled water with salt. Then he was given boiled water with sugar. Mother alternated this every few hours.

She wouldn't let anyone help her.

"No," she told Father, "the fewer people who come near him the less chance of everyone getting it. If I need you I'll holler."

James got worse as the day passed. That night, Warren and William came down with the infection. Father brought them over to Mother's camp and stayed with them.

"I'm staying Rachel." Joseph heard his Father say. "Don't argue with me. You can't tend to three sick boys by yourself."

"All right." Mother said. She knew a lot about cholera. Her father, Dr. Bly, had instructed her. She learned from him especially after she had overcome the disease herself. Grandfather Bly felt the main thing was to keep everything clean. Boiling and burning, he called it. Boil everything you eat or drink and burn anything that touches the sickness. Keep your hands clean too. Her father was laughed at by many, including other doctors, but his patients seem to survive more often that other doctors'

"You'll have to do exactly as I tell you Samuel. We can't have you getting sick."

Joseph watched as Father gave Mother a hug. Joseph was so worried about his little brothers. Joseph thought, This is just another reason why we should have stayed home At home the boys wouldn't have gotten sick, and if they had, Grandmother and Grandfather Bly would have helped Mother.

Joseph stayed up late and wrote by the firelight:

> *The little ones are sick. I'm worried about them.*
> *I wish that we were home. I'm praying that they'll*
> *be all right.*

Mother and Father stayed up day and night tending to the boys. When Jane came down with the sickness, Moses brought her and the baby over. He stayed. Father couldn't persuade him to leave.

"If Jane and the baby die, Mr. Samuel, I might as well die too." Moses said as he wiped Jane's head with a clean cloth. The sickness lasted for seven days. On the seventh day, James lifted his head and said, "Mother could I have some johnny cake please?' Mother took his frail little body in her arms and laughed and cried at the same time.

"Thank you, thank you, thank you." Joseph repeated to anyone who was listening. He did a little dancing jig in celebration of Jamie's recovery.

The other sick ones were slowly recovering too, all except Jane who seemed to get weaker each day.

Joseph went into the woods and kneeled down and folded his hands. "Dear Lord, Joseph said aloud. He prayed while looking up at the sky. "You heard me before. I'll make a deal with you. I won't complain and ask to go home anymore if you'll just make Jane better. Moses and Abraham need her. I don't think Moses can make it without Jane. You can make me sick in her place. Just please make her well. Amen." Joseph heard footsteps behind him and looked.

"You shouldn't make bargains with God, Joseph. He might just take you up on it. And then where would we be? We'd have you getting sick." Isaac said to his little brother. "You can't make deals with God, Joseph. He does what he does and it isn't our place to question it."

Joseph hung his head in front of his brother. As soon as Isaac walked away he looked up towards the sky. "I mean it Lord. Please make Jane well. Amen, " he whispered.

Jane didn't get well. Her body seemed to shrink. Her face turned an awful gray color with a blue cast to it, and her eyes looked like they were lying in craters. She faded in and out of consciousness.

Joseph and everyone else kept praying for Jane. The other sick ones slowly regained their strength and began to sit up in their beds.

Late on the eighth night, Mother was tending to Jane. She was washing her face when Jane looked at her.

"I want to see my baby," she croaked. "please let me hold my baby."

"I'm sorry Jane. " Mother said gently. "But I can't risk you giving the baby the sickness. You're just going to have to get well to see him."

A stubborn look came into Jane's sunken eyes. A spark flashed in her brown eyes.

"I will get better!" she rasped out. "You'll see." She went back to sleep, but it seemed to be a more natural sleep and she didn't seem to be withdrawing anymore.

On the ninth day of the family's sickness, Father went into the nearest town to get a doctor. Mother had exhausted her medicinal supplies and she wanted a doctor to see Jane. It was risky with the slave catchers active in the area, but there was no other choice.

Joseph watched Father go and wished that he could go with him. Father could put him on the stage for home. But, since he had made his bargain with God and Jane seemed to be getting better, he wasn't sure that he could go now.

Joseph felt very warm. He started to feel really sick to his stomach. All of a sudden he needed to relieve himself. He barely made it to the bushes behind the wagon. After he was through his stomach felt like it was on fire. He was so weak his legs could hardly hold him up.

"Mother!" he called weakly. "Somebody help me." His voice was barely above a whisper, but David heard him and came around the side of the wagon.

"Oh no!" David cried as he scooped Joseph up. "Not Joseph too. When will this end? Mother come quick! It's Joseph. He's got the sickness."

Mother ran across the road. She felt Joseph's head and took one look and shook her head. "I had hoped that he would escape this time."

Joseph knew he had the cholera. He knew why too. God had answered his prayer. Not only did he have cholera, he couldn't go home. He was stuck. It made him feel sicker.

"Mother please help me. I feel awful sick." Joseph cried pitifully. He had never felt so awful in his whole life. He messed his pants over and over. The first time it happened he was humiliated and begged Mother not to tell anyone. After that, he didn't care. He had no control over his body what so ever. After a while he started to vomit. He vomited until there was nothing left and then he did some more. He felt like his insides had turned outside. Then, he noticed that Mother was sort of fuzzy looking. He couldn't really see her clearly anymore. His lips were so dry and he tried to talk but the words wouldn't come. Then the world went black and he didn't see anything. Then, there was a bright light shining all around him. "Mother?" he called. "Mother where are you?" No one answered him. He did feel warm and cozy though and it seemed like someone was holding him and rocking him gently.

"Joseph! Joseph, open your eyes. " He opened his eyes and saw Father and Mother looking down at him. He saw sunlight filtering through the tent opening. His eyes felt like heavy weights and his body was so tired.

"The doctor was here Joseph. He said that you and Jane are going to get well. You must drink lots of water, dear, so take this now." Mother said as she held a cup for Joseph to drink from. It was some of her willow bark tea. It tasted wonderful. He was so thirsty.

"The doctor told Mother that she saved all of your lives with her nursing. He said that he couldn't have done a better job. So, you're in good hands son. Just get stronger every day so that we can get on our way. If you still want to go back to live with Grandmother Bly you can. You'll just have to wait until you're much better. We can't send you back sick now, can we?" Father said. He held Joseph up while Mother fed him and then bathed him.

Joseph was weary but he was glad to see his parents again. He was glad to be alive. And happy that he was getting well. He'd worry about going back home tomorrow. Today it didn't seem so important. It felt mighty good just being held in Father's strong arms.

"What day is this Mother?" Joseph asked.

"It's Tuesday. You have been sick for a week."

"A week!" Joseph said. He was surprised. He couldn't believe that he'd been sick for a week. It seemed like it was yesterday that he'd started feeling bad.

Joseph started to feel more like himself every day. Friday, he got out of bed. He tried walking around on Saturday. His legs were wobbly and he got tired very quickly.

On Sunday, Father had a prayer service to give thanks that everyone was well again. Then, they had a picnic and played games.

Joseph wrote:

> *I was sick with cholera. It was terrible. I'm glad to be well again.*
>
> *I still want to go back to Virginia, but I want to stay with my family too.*
>
> *I don't know what to do.*

CHAPTER SEVEN

Crossing The Ohio

The family got back on the road early Monday morning. They had lost two weeks with the cholera outbreak.

Joseph, riding in the wagon with Jane and the babies heard Mother and Father talking.

"We have lost so much time Rachel. Now we won't get to Indiana before October. We won't have time to plant any crops and our money is running out. I had to pay the doctor and buy more supplies when everyone was sick. What are we going to do? We could go back home and try again next year. Your mother would share the profits from the farm with us."

Joseph held his breath. Go back home? His prayers would be answered. Mother quickly dashed those hopes.

"Don't be silly, Samuel. I never knew that you were a quitter. It will be harder, but we didn't expect it to be easy this year did we? I'm not going back. Ike will help us. You'll see."

Father's face was drawn and wrinkles had creased his forehead. He kissed Mother on the cheek and rode off to scout the road ahead. After he left, Joseph saw Mother's shoulders sag just for a moment. Then, she straightened up, tossed back her head and went on with her chores.

Maybe Father will decide to go back home anyway. Joseph hoped. I wonder if I could persuade Mother to agree with Father and then….. we could be back home for Christmas. Yes, that's exactly what I'll do. Joseph made some plans.

"Mother," Joseph said as they were riding down the road later that morning. "Aren't you worried about getting to Indiana late in the year? We won't have any time to plant crops and harvest them."

"Yes, son I am. But we have brought many supplies with us. Your father is a good hunter and I know your Uncle Ike will help us. At least the Ike I used to know would help us." Mother said. There was just a trace of doubt in Mother's voice which Joseph caught.

"But Mother, what if he's changed and doesn't want to help us?" Joseph asked with pretended innocence.

"Then we'll manage somehow. Now, you take a rest son. You're not completely well yet." The doubt was still in his mother's voice.

Joseph hunkered down under the covers and thought with a smile on his face I think we'll be going home soon.

"Joseph wake up. You've been sleeping all afternoon." James and Warren were shaking him awake.

"What's the matter?" he asked sleepily.

" Nothing. Mother wants you to get up to eat some supper. We stopped for the night an hour ago."

Joseph got out of the wagon and sat down by the fire. His mother handed him a plate of beans and bread. Everyone else was almost finished eating. Father stood up.

"We're going to start traveling longer hours now. We have to get to Indiana as soon as we can so that we will get settled by the first snow. It's going to be hard, but I know that each of you can do it. Mother is going to start rationing our supplies from now on too. There will be plenty of food, but it won't be fancy. I'm going to take David and Isaac hunting tomorrow to see if we can't get something that we can smoke and use to make jerky."

David and Isaac hooted with excitement. They raced to get their guns to clean and load. Joseph was discouraged. He needed to talk to

Father soon or his plans could go wrong. Besides, he hated jerky. The idea of living off cooked leather for the rest of the trip really increased his desire to go back to Virginia.

Father walked to the edge of the camp and lit his pipe. Joseph followed.

"Joseph, what are you up to now?" his father said.

"Why Father, I just wanted to be with you." he replied. " I do have something on my mind Father, but I don't know if I should tell you or not." He looked up at his father carefully to see his expression.

"Go on son. Is this about going home again?"

"No. It's about Mother."

"Your Mother? What about your Mother?"

"Mother's worried about going to Indiana, but she's afraid to tell you. She doesn't think Ike will help us and she doesn't think we'll have enough food. You won't tell her I told you will you Father? She told me not to tell you because she didn't want me to worry you. I just thought that you ought to know." Joseph said. He finished his white lies and felt guilty.

Father looked at him intently. He studied Joseph so carefully that Joseph was afraid that he could see into his mind. He took a puff on his pipe and turned around. He stood with his back to Joseph.

"Hmm. I thought that she was hiding something from me this morning. Thank you for telling me Joseph. I think I need to have a talk with her. Maybe we'll all go back home together. That would make you happy, wouldn't it Joseph?"

"Yes sir." Joseph replied trying not to sound too excited. "I'm going to bed now Father. I'm awfully tired."

"Goodnight son." Father said. He watched his son walk back to the wagon with a spring to his step. Father smiled with a knowing look in his eyes.

"Rachel," Father said, "why don't we take a little walk down the road here?"

"I'd love to dear." Mother replied.

The couple walked side by side in comfortable silence for a few minutes. Father cleared his throat and began to speak.

"Rachel in all the years that we've been married we've been honest with each other, haven't we?"

"Of course, Samuel. I've tried to be honest with you, and I believe that you have been straightforward with me. Why are you asking me this? Is something bothering you?"

Mother asked. She watched with concern as Father pulled absently on his dark beard.

"Do you remember our conversation this morning, Rachel?"

"Of course, dear."

"Well, I have been informed that you no longer want to continue our journey. I have been told that you want to go back home. I now know that you don't trust Ike anymore to help us when we get to Indiana. Why didn't you tell me this morning my dear?"

Mother was so shocked and outraged that she didn't see the teasing glint in Father's eyes as he finished his speech.

"Why Samuel Harding, you know that's not true. What I told you this morning was exactly what I meant. I haven't changed my mind at all. I have always supported you in this move. You know that. How could you doubt me? I have never lied to you and for you to accuse me of such a thing is preposterous. I'm outraged. I'm …." Mother said.

Mother was at a loss for words because she was so upset. She turned to stride back to the camp when Father caught her arm. She turned angrily and faced him.

"Before you really get on your high horse Rachel, think a minute. Who did you talk to after I left you this morning? What did you say?" Father probed.

"I talked to Jane about Mary and then Joseph started to ask me a lot of questions about what you and I discussed. I expressed my worries, but I never said I wanted to go back home or that I didn't trust Ike. Wait a minute! Do you mean to tell me that, that little…" Mother said as she began to understand what Father wanted her to see.

"Oh, wait till I get my hands on that son of ours. Joseph won't be sitting down for a week. He really thought that if you believed that I wanted to go home we would. He played on our worries for his own selfish desires."

"Actually, it was very clever Rachel. He just twisted a few of your statements and embellished them a little and presented them to me thinking that I would go along with his plan. He probably expects that by tomorrow we'll be heading back to Virginia. Unfortunately for him, I saw through him from the beginning. He doesn't realize how well I know you. It's very selfish I agree, but young boys are very selfish. It's natural. Let's play along with this and teach him a lesson about selfishness. This what we're going to do." Father told Mother his plan. She started to chuckle and they both walked back to camp with smiles on their faces. They were holding hands.

Joseph watched his parents return and smiled to himself. Tomorrow they would start back home. He was certain of it. He wanted to write in his diary but he didn't want his parents to see him. Oh well, he could write tomorrow while they were traveling back home. T.B. was curled up next to him and he put his arm around the hound and sighed happily and went to sleep.

At breakfast Father looked at Mother. She nodded her head slightly. Father stood up. Everyone stopped eating. They knew by now that when Father stood up he was going to tell them something important. The whole group watched him expectantly.

Father cleared his throat. He put his hands on his suspenders and pulled on them. Then he rocked back on his heels.

"It has come to my attention that some of you do not want to continue our journey. I have learned that a few of you would like to go back home." Father looked pointedly at Mother and Joseph. Joseph squirmed. Mother ducked her head to hide her smiles.

Everyone else looked at Father in disbelief. They looked at each other. Then everyone but Joseph looked back at Father in puzzlement.

"Who wants to go back Father? It's surely not me." David exclaimed."And I know Isaac wants to go on. He and I have already planned the farm we're going to build together."

"That's right, Father." Isaac confirmed. "And I know that John is anxious to go to Indiana too. He told me so."

"I can hardly wait to get there Father." John stood up and gestured toward the west. "I want to be a pioneer and settle a new land like you did when you were a boy."

"Me too, Father." Warren interrupted. "I want to go with you and Mother. Don't leave me behind. Don't send me back. Please Father."

"Oh don't be so bawly, Warren," said John, who thought Warren was being silly.

Father patted Warren on the head and glowered at John. "Don't worry, Warren. We couldn't go on without you."

"Father, " James began, "I want to go with you too. I want to see Uncle Ike. Mother says he's real nice."

Joseph groaned inwardly. James and Mother were the only ones he thought that he could count on to help him win everyone over. Now James had betrayed him. Only Mother was left. He looked hopefully at her. Mother looked back at Joseph. She looked at the other faces. Then she looked at Father.

"Well, my dear?" Father asked. "Are you the one who wants to go back home?"

"No. Someone misunderstood me. I was voicing some concerns I had and he understood those statements to mean that I wanted to go home. Let everyone understand me here and now. I did not want to leave my home and family, but I knew that we could not live in Virginia anymore. I also trust my husband. I know that he would not take us somewhere where we wouldn't prosper." Mother looked sternly at Joseph. "Someone twisted my words and told Father I wanted to go home. I'm sure that he didn't mean to do any harm." Mother finished and sat down.

"I want to ask Moses, Jane, and Ben if they want to continue with us." Father looked at the three in question.

"Yes. We want to continue. I'm speaking for Jane and myself. You know that we can't go back. Our only hope for a better life is in the north. If we went back they would take Abraham away from us." Moses put a protective arm around his wife.

"I'm with you, too, Mr. Samuel. There's nothing for me back in Virginia. I'm hoping to make a new start in Indiana. I'm just grateful to you and Miss Rachel for taking me with you." Ben said.

A loud "whoof" came from T.B.

"Well, I guess we know how he feels." Father laughed. Then his face became serious again. "That leaves only one of us left. Joseph, do you want to say something?"

Joseph felt his face grow hot. He squirmed and wiggled. He couldn't meet anyone's eyes. He knew that Father was waiting for an answer, but he didn't know how to begin.

"Joseph?" Father was getting impatient. He was tapping his foot against the wagon wheel as he put his large hands on Joseph's shoulders, forcing him to look up.

"I a...I'm sorry Father. I still want to go back to Virginia, but I didn't mean to make trouble for you and Mother."

"Well, you did young man. You should be punished, but instead your Mother and I have decided that if you are that determined to go home then we will let you go. However, we do not have the money for the stage. You will have to catch a ride with someone heading in that direction. You will probably have to walk for part of the way too. Are you willing to do that to get back home? Do you want to go home that much?"

No stage? Walking? Joseph considered this. He really wanted to go home, but riding with someone else or walking didn't appeal to him one bit.

"Have you made a decision?" Father asked.

"No. May I think about it for awhile? Can I let you know tonight, Father?"

"That will be fine with me, but we are traveling on. If you decide to leave it will be that many more miles that you have to travel to go back."

"I know. But I want to think about it for awhile. Maybe someone will come along that I can ride back with all the way."

"That's fine Joseph, but remember this also. If you should decide to stay with us there will be no more complaining or talk of going back. You will also receive a punishment for trying to come between your Mother and myself. Do you understand?"

"Yes sir." Joseph agreed solemnly.

The family got ready to travel. None of his brothers spoke to Joseph. They gave him mean looks , however, that told him how they each felt.

Isaac looked at him with disappointment. He made Joseph feel like he had betrayed Isaac's trust. David gave him a disgusted look that said he didn't want anything to do with him.

John was the only one who finally talked to him. "What are you up to?" he hissed at Joseph. "Are you addleheaded? What's wrong with you anyway? Don't you want to live with your family? You don't care about anyone but yourself, Joseph. You're selfish. That's exactly what you are…. A selfish piece of nothing. I'm not speaking to you ever again as long as I live!" John stomped off to help Father hitch up the horses. The little boys looked at their older brother with hurt in their eyes.

"Don't you like us anymore?" William asked.

"Why don't you want to be with us?"

"Well, if you don't like us, we don't like you!" cried James. The other two nodded their heads in agreement. They turned their backs on Joseph and went to help Mother with Mary.

Even the dog growled at him when he bent down to pat it on the head.

Moses and Jane didn't say anything to him. They didn't have to. He could sense their disapproval without any words being said. Ben did not come near him.

Moses and Jane got into their secret compartment. They were going to be traveling near a town today and they didn't want to take any chances.

The weather was horrid. It was damp and cloudy. It started to mist and then drizzle about midmorning.

Great. Joseph thought as he walked along beside the wagon. Pulling his rain slicker close about him he trudged along in the mud. Mother had invited him into the wagon, but he didn't feel very welcome there. The younger boys were in there and they weren't speaking to him. He walked alone. No one came near him. He talked to himself since there was no one else.

The rain sure fits my mood today. What am I going to do? I want to go back home, but not in someone else's wagon and I sure don't want to walk by myself. I'll say it. I would be scared to walk in the woods by myself. If I stay, everyone will hate me and Father will probably tie me to a wagon wheel for days. I'll get no water or food and then I'd die. Then everyone would feel sorry They'd miss me too. Joseph had worked himself up into a high state of self-pity. He seemed to forget who brought his misery on. He continued to feel sorry for himself for the rest of the day. The rain started to come down in sheets so Mother pulled the wagon over. Father and the older boys got into the wagon with everyone else. Joseph was pulled into the wagon by Father.

"We don't need you getting sick again."

Joseph sat huddled in the wagon. Everyone seemed to enjoy being together in the cramped, small space. Mother got out some dried fruit and passed it around. Joseph refused the fruit. Then, Father started singing and everyone joined in. Everyone that is except Joseph. He still continued to be alone with his whole family around him.

The wind started to rock the wagon gently back and forth. Father got out of the wagon and unhitched the secret compartment. "No use you three staying in there. I doubt any slave catchers are on the road today. Come and get in the wagon. I'm going to unhitch the horses. I don't think we're going to get anymore traveling done today. Not with this storm picking up." Moses and Jane scrambled into the wagon with the baby as Father and Ben unhitched the horses, fed them, and tied them up. David and Isaac got out of the wagon and helped Father tie the wagon down in case the wind got any stronger.

The storm continued throughout the evening. Mother served a cold supper which was washed down with water. Everyone scrunched down to sleep as best they could. The wagon was packed tighter than a chinked cabin.

"This is real cozy Mother." James said as Mother tucked him in. "I like everyone sleeping together. It makes me happy."

"Once in awhile it's good to be close to your family James, but I don't think you'd like to do this every night. Just like everything else you'd get tired of it. Good night, dear." Mother said as she kissed James and moved to tuck in the other boys.

"What about you, Joseph? You've been awfully quiet today? Have you come to a decision yet?" Mother asked as she pulled the covers up to his chin.

"I believe I wanted an answer tonight son." Father said. "But since this has been an unusual night we'll let it go until morning. Goodnight."

Joseph lay on his pallet thinking. He hated to admit it, but he too had enjoyed being with his family in the wagon tonight. He felt torn between two wants. He wanted to go back to Virginia, but he also wanted to stay with his parents and brothers and Mary. He couldn't sleep. He listened to the wind and rain as it surrounded the wagon. He listened to the others as they made sleep noises. He heard his father softly snoring. He was beginning to doze off when he was brought awake with a jerk. Something had hit the wagon. Then he felt another thud. Joseph peered outside. He immediately went to his Father.

"Father! Father wake up! The creek, the creek!" He cried. Father sat up rubbing sleep from his eyes.

"What? Oh, it's you Joseph. What do you want?"

"Father the creek is rising. The creek is like a river!"

Father jerked off the bedclothes and leaped to the wagon's opening. He looked outside. He couldn't believe his eyes.

"Great Tarnation!" he exclaimed . "Rachel! Children! Everyone wake up. The creek bed has flooded and we're about to be swept away. Everyone get up. We've go to move this wagon to higher ground before we lose it. Hurry! We have no time to lose." Father jumped to the ground as he spoke. He was running toward the horses.

"David! Isaac! Ben! You come and help me get these horses hitched to the wagon." David and Isaac were already out of the wagon before Father had finished. Ben was pulling the wagon tongue out of the sandy bottom of the swollen creek bed.

"Children, Moses, Jane! You get out of the wagon and wait over there on that hill. I'll get some supplies out." Mother said as she started to carry bedding and food out of the wagon. Moses and all of the others disregarded her orders. They, too, helped to get the precious supplies out of wagon. If they lost the wagon, they didn't want to lose their supplies.

Jane carried the two babies over to the hill and tended to them. She was trying to keep them dry and warm.

"Be gentle now, boys." Father told his two oldest sons. "These horses are frightened by the storm. We can't afford to have them bolt on us now. We need them too badly. " Heeding Father's advice, David and Isaac held the horses bridles firmly, but gently and guided them over to the wagon. The wind pulled at their clothes and the rain blinded them as they settled the horses in front of the wagon. The creek was filling up at an alarming rate. There was not a moment to spare.

Mother, Moses, and the children had finished unloading as much as they could. They ran for the hillside where Jane was huddled. T.B. brought up the rear. He carried an extra blanket in his mouth which he dropped down in front of Jane. Jane patted the dog on his head and took the much needed cover for the babies.

Joseph watched with his stomach in his throat as the men tried to get the horses harnessed to the wagon while the water rose around them. The current seemed to increasing and it was becoming more difficult for the men to stay on their feet. Out of the corner of his eye Joseph saw a tree limb traveling swiftly by him. It was going down the creek bed heading straight for the men. It was aiming to hit Isaac in the back of the leg as he struggled to get Dobbin's last harness buckled.

"Isaac watch out! Look behind you!" Joseph screamed at his brother. Isaac looked behind. Horror crossed his face and for a split second he froze. Then he dodged under Dobbin's body. The limb missed him by an inch. Isaac came out from under the horse's belly and wiped his brow. He looked up toward the hill and gave Joseph a grateful smile. He waved to Joseph, who waved back. He was joyful that Isaac had not been hit.

Father and the boys got the wagon hitched and carefully guided the horses out of the creek and up the hill. Inch by inch they climbed until they were finally out of danger. Everyone gave a cheer. When the wagon was sitting next to them on the hillside. Joseph cheered louder than anyone.

Isaac grabbed Joseph and hugged him so hard the air was squeezed out of him.

"Thanks little brother. You saved my life. If that limb had hit me, I'd have been a goner." Isaac said. Isaac gave him another squeeze.

Father took Joseph from Isaac and tossed him up in the air. He put him on his wide shoulders. "This is the hero of the day everyone. If Joseph hadn't awakened me we'd all be going down river by now. We'd have surely lost the wagon and who knows what else. We all owe a great deal to Joseph. Let's give him a great big hurrah. Everyone! Hurrah!" Everyone yelled. Mother and Jane gave him a big kiss and all of his brothers hugged him. Even the babies smiled and cooed. T.B. slurped him in the face with his big, pink tongue.

Joseph laughed and smiled. He felt funny inside. "Aw, anybody else would have done the same thing." He said as his face blushed.

"Yes, but Joseph you're not just anybody. You're the one who wanted to go back home, remember? If the wagon had been lost with all of our supplies, we would have been forced to go back to Virginia. Did you think of that, son?" Father asked.

"I didn't think Father. I was just so scared when the wagon started moving that all I could do was get you up. Really Father, I didn't think of anything else."

"Look there everyone." Father pointed toward the sky. The sun was just rising and with it came a beautiful rainbow. "I think this a sign for us all. Let's give thanks that Joseph woke up and warned us before it was too late." Everyone, including Joseph, bowed his head in silent prayer.

Joseph prayed silently. Thank you God, for helping me help my family. Now I don't know what I want. I would like to go back to Virginia, but I don't want to leave everyone. They need me just as I need them. Help me decide what to do. Amen. Joseph looked up to see all of his family looking at him.

"Well, Joseph what's it to be? We need to be going. Are you going with us or are you heading back to Virginia?" Father asked.

"I'd like to keep going with you and the family for now Father. If you don't mind. I'm still not sure about this move, but I know I don't want to leave right now. Maybe later on. I'll go back later."

"Fine. But remember no more complaining or manipulating. Is that understood?"

"Yes sir. But what does manipulating mean?"

"What you tried with your Mother and me."

"Oh. What's my punishment Father?"

"I think after last night we'll forgo the punishment for right now. That is if you mean what you say."

"I do Father. If I have any complaining, I'll talk to myself or T.B.. He listens, but he doesn't repeat much." T.B. stuck his muzzle under Joseph's hand as if in agreement.

"Good. Then, I think we need to get on our way. We have a long way to go and a very short time to get there."

After a quick breakfast, the wagon party was on their way. The weather favored them for the next few weeks and they made good time. They pulled in to Huntington on August 27, 1850. Father bought some essential supplies such as flour and salt, but no extras. Joseph and his brothers walked around the town while their father and mother shopped. Huntington had a main street that was busy with wagons and carriages. The dirt rose up like a dust storm each time a wagon or carriage passed the boys. There were many shops along the street. The boys peered into each one as they walked slowly down the board covered walkway.

Joseph saw Mother beckon to them so he and his brothers headed back to the wagon.

Father was very excited when they got to the wagon. "There's a ferry here." He told the children. "It's not expensive either. For some reason the gold fever folks haven't come to Huntington yet. I want to get on the other side of the Ohio River before they do. Let's go!"

The ferry was on the south side of town. The owner was a Mr. Smith and his two grown sons. He took the fare from Father and motioned for Mother to bring the wagon onto the ferry. This was something that the children had never done before. Joseph and John hung over the railing and watched the swirls of the Ohio River pass before them. Warren and James stayed in the wagon with Mother.

"I don't want to have to fish you boys out of the river. You're going to stay right here with me." She said firmly with an arm around each child.

"I can't understand how they pull this wagon across." William asked his Father. Father held him up and pointed to the other side. "See those horses pulling that rope?" William nodded. "Well, the rope is attached to a pulley. The pulley is attached to the ferry and the horses and the pulley bring the wagon across. The horses on the other side will take it back to Mr. Smith when we get off." William sort of understood.

Joseph thought it was wonderful. He could have floated all the way down river on the ferry. However, the ride was over very quickly. Mother, with Father's help guided the wagon off the ferry. David and Isaac brought the riding horses off. Ben brought Ellie, the cow. Father had traded one of the horses for Ellie in Huntington. It was a good trade, and Ellie would be necessary when they got to their farm.

The wagon rolled down the road for about half an hour. Father stopped abruptly. "Rachel stop. Do you realize where we are? We're halfway to Indiana. It's a free state. We can let Moses and Jane out of the hiding place for awhile each day."

"Are you sure, dear? Can't slave catchers take them back even if they're in a free state?"

"Yes, but we'll be very careful. We'll keep them in the wagon most of the day. It just seems so cruel to make them stay in that compartment all day especially now that we're in Ohio."

"I agree. Let's take a chance."

Joseph wrote in his diary:

> *Today we went across the river on a ferry. Now we are in Ohio. We are farther away from Virginia.*

CHAPTER EIGHT

Traveling In Ohio

Now that they were in Ohio the whole family felt like Indiana was almost within reach. Joseph had mixed feelings. He was happy that they were almost in Indiana, but he still missed his old home. He still wanted to go back to Virginia. He would keep the promise that he made to Father. He wouldn't do anymore pranks to get them to go back home.

Of course, he thought, if something happened that made Father want to turn around and go back home, I wouldn't say no.

As they wound their way through southern Ohio Joseph noticed black people working in the fields.

"Father, I thought that Ohio was a free state. Why are there Negroes working in the fields?" Joseph asked his father.

"They could be free men, Joseph , working for wages or they could be slaves who were brought up here by former southerners. Remember we are in Southern Ohio. We'll have to watch what we say until we get farther north."

They traveled along the river under the hot August sun. There had been no rain since the night of the flooded creek so they had to make do with muddy river water. Mother boiled the water before using it to cook with or to drink.

Joseph walked along beside the wagon with his brothers most of the time now. He enjoyed being outside the wagon. He felt as strong now as he had before the cholera.

About a week after they had crossed the Ohio, they came upon what seemed to be an abandoned farm. Father approached the house, but it seemed that no one was home. The house was boarded up and the grass had overgrown the garden next to the back door. Mother wouldn't let Father get water from the well.

"You never know Samuel. The well could have gone bad. Unless we know that it's safe I don't want to risk the sickness again."

As they were just about to leave the farm yard, they heard a feeble cry for help. It seemed to be coming from inside the house. Father pried open the door and went inside. Quickly, he came back outside.

"Rachel, come quick. There's a woman inside. She seems very sick."

Mother hurried into the house. Joseph followed with the medicine basket.

"Help me. Please." A feeble voice rasped from a bed in the corner. It was hard to see the face that belonged to the voice. The woman's frail, tiny, white body seemed enveloped in the covers on the bed.

"Of course we'll help. What are you doing here by yourself in this abandoned house?" Mother asked the old woman.

"I put the boards up two weeks ago when a bad storm was brewing. Then, when the storm hit, I was caught outside. A tree limb hit me and I barely made it into the house. I haven't been well since. Usually, my neighbors next door help me out. They come by every week or so to see me. But they haven't been by since my accident. I hope nothing has happened to them."

The old woman tried to get up, but she groaned in pain and fell back onto the bed.

"It's my right shoulder and my arm." She said in agony.

"Let's take a look at them." Mother said gently. She gently touched the old lady's shoulder. The woman turned as white as the sheet and grimaced with pain. "I see what the problem is. Your shoulder is dislocated. We need to get it back into the socket. This is going to hurt like the devil, but once I'm done you should start to feel better." As Mother talked to the woman she firmly but carefully grabbed the frail arm and pulled it with a jerking motion. The woman gasped and fell backwards in a dead faint. Joseph held his breath. He saw the woman's chest rise and fall so he knew that she was still alive.

"We'll camp here for the night and help her." Father said and Mother nodded in agreement. Mother began to tidy up the small, frame house as Father went out to the wagon. Joseph saw Father talk with the others. Father got Moses, Jane and the baby out of the wagon's false bottom. Father told Moses and Jane what was happening inside. They decided to stay inside the wagon just to be on the safe side. The children began to do the chores that were necessary for the evening camp. Inside the house, Mother found some pots and pans in the lady's kitchen.

"Joseph go out to the wagon and get me some potatoes, onions, and beans. I'll cook on a real stove tonight in a house with a roof over my head. What a treat." Mother said. Smiling, Mother hummed to herself as she went to work in the kitchen.

As Joseph came into the house with Mother's supplies, he saw that the lady was awake again. She was looking around puzzled and confused about what was going on or where she was.

"Mother the lady is awake." Joseph said.

"Oh, how wonderful." Mother said as she walked over to the bed and felt the wrinkled forehead. "Good. There doesn't seem to be any fever at the moment. How do you feel now? Do you remember me? My family and I discovered you a little while ago. You hurt your shoulder and I fixed it."

"I remember now. My arm feels so much better. I think I can get up. What must you think of me? Here you are guests in my house and I'm lying in bed. If you'll just help me get up." The old woman started to get out of the bed. Mother stopped her.

"Now, don't be foolish. You need to rest that shoulder. You can begin to get up in a day or so when you're stronger." Mother helped the woman to sit up in bed. She plumped the pillows and placed them behind the lady's white head.

"Maybe you're right. You're so kind to help an old lady like me. Oh, forgive my manners. I haven't introduced myself. My name is Mary Ruth Walden. My husband and I have lived on this farm for thirty years. We had three children, but they died of the fever when they were babies. My husband, Jesse, died four years ago. It's been hard to farm and keep things up since he died. I've just about decided to sell this place and move into town. I have a niece that lives there. She's been begging me to come live with her. My gracious! Listen to me rattle on. When you live by yourself you do rattle on when there's someone to talk to." Mrs. Walden extended her arm and pointed a frail, clawlike, finger to Joseph. He backed up without thinking. "And who might you be, young man?" She asked.

"Mrs. Walden, this is our son Joseph. My name is Rachel Harding and my husband, Samuel is the man who found you today. Our family is moving to Indiana to farm.

"How nice dear. You know when I first saw your husband I thought it was my Jesse coming for me. He favors Jesse y'know. I want to thank him. Where is the rest of your family? Can you stay and rest here for awhile? It would truly pleasure me to have you keep me company?"

"We're happy to be here." Mother said as she bustled about the kitchen. "We plan to spend the night if you don't mind. I wanted to fix you a hot meal and make sure you don't develop a fever. I also want my husband to notify your neighbors and your niece so that someone can look in on you. Actually, you're doing me a favor. This is the first time I've been able to cook inside for two months. This is very exciting for me."

"I seem to be awfully tired." Mrs. Walden fell asleep on the last word.

"Joseph, go get Father and tell him to come in here," Mother instructed. Joseph ran outside eager to explore the small farm.

"Father, Mother wants you. The lady's name is Mrs. Walden and she's lived here for . . ."

"Whoa, son. Slow down. Let me go see what Mother wants. You help your brothers set up camp for the night."

"Yes, sir," replied Joseph as he headed for the barn.

Father went into the house. He carried a small ham that he had found in a smokehouse behind the barn.

"Rachel, do you think that you can use this tonight? I thought maybe the lady could use the nourishment of meat with her meal. Do you think the well is safe? It sure would be nice to have a cold drink of well water, wouldn't it? I'm sorry, dear. Joseph told me to come in. Did you need something?"

"It's my turn to talk, Samuel," Mother said. "You sounded just like Joseph. Did Joseph tell you about Mrs. Walden?"

"He started to, but I wanted him to help with the chores. What's the story?"

Mother quickly filled in the details. "Can you go to the neighbors and tell them what happened? Maybe they can send someone into town for the niece. She really needs someone to stay here and look after her. This farm is really too much for a woman her age. I hope she does sell it and move into town. She's going to need someone keeping an eye on her for some time."

"I'm on my way. I saw chimney smoke about a mile up the road. I may take one of the boys with me. We'll be back soon." Father gave Mother a quick hug and headed out of the door.

The first child he saw was Joseph who was drawing pictures in the dirt. "Are those chores done, Joseph?"

"No, sir," Joseph said. "But everyone else has something to do. No one wanted my help."

"All right. Then, you can come with me. We're going to find the neighbors and tell them about Mrs. Walden."

Father and Joseph mounted the horse and rode off together. Joseph rode behind Father holding on to his waist.

As they went down the road, Joseph saw a small grove of trees with a fence around it. Inside the fence were four graves. Joseph felt sad when he saw it. There was the woman's whole family under those trees. She really was all alone.

Father saw a lane up ahead on the right. "I'll bet that's where her neighbors are. Let's go see."

A two-story house sat at the end of the lane. As they approached, a woman came out of the front door wiping her hands on a snowy white apron.

"Hello there," she called. "How can I help you, today?"

"Hello, ma'am. My name is Samuel Harding. This is my son Joseph. We've just come from Mrs. Walden's house. She was hurt in that storm awhile back and needed some help. My family and I happened to ride by and hear her cries for help. She was wondering if you could send someone to town for her niece. We plan to stay the night, but we must be on our way tomorrow."

"Oh, dear. I feel just awful. I should have gone over there as soon as the storm was over, but my husband and oldest boy took sick and I've been nursing them. I'll send one of our boys into town right away. You tell Mary I'll be over first thing in the morning to stay until her niece gets there. My name is Helen Morgan. It's a pleasure to meet you. Won't you stay for supper?"

"No, Ma'am. Thank you just the same. My wife has our meal started back at Mrs. Walden's. We'll see you in the morning then. Good day."

"Yes, I'll be there first thing. I'm just happy that you came by to help her. Good bye."

Father and Joseph rode back to Mrs. Walden's house.

"Father, go faster."

You want to go fast, do you? Well, let's see if old' Fire here wants to take you faster. How about it, Fire? Do you want to go faster?"

Fire tossed his head and headed down the road at a gallop. His brown mane was blown by the wind.

Joseph grasped his Father's waist and hung on for dear life. It was wonderful! The wind rushed through his hair and seemed to pull him from Father. He could feel the horses muscles bunch underneath him and he listened to the clopping sound Fire's hooves made as he sped down the road. They seemed to be back at Mrs. Walden's house in no time at all. Joseph was sorry the ride was over so soon.

"Father! I didn't know Fire could run so fast."

"Fire was once used for racing, son. That was before we got him, but he still has a race or two left in him, I guess, don't you old' boy?" Father gave Fire a pat and then took the saddle and blanket off of the horse's back.

"Go rub him down in the barn, Joseph, and give him an extra scoop of fee."

Yes, sir." Joseph answered his father.

"Come on, Fire. Let's go get you comfortable," Joseph said as he walked the

Father went into the little white house. "Rachel, I'm back. Mrs. Morgan from next door is coming over in the morning, and she's sending someone into town to find brown stallion to the barn. Fire was nodding his head in agreement.Mrs. Walden's niece."

"I heard you coming, Samuel. I was worried something was wrong until I looked out and saw the smiles on your faces. You and Joseph had some ride back, didn't you?

Father grinned sheepishly. "Joseph wanted to go faster."

"And you always do what Joseph wants? Hmm. Who really wanted to go faster? You or your son?" Mother said with her hands on her hips. There was a teasing glint in her eyes. She chuckled softly and then said, "Why don't you take down the boards over the windows? Maybe you can get some of the children to cut back the weeds in the yard for Mrs. Walden. I'm sure that it would perk her up to see the yard looking tidy. Supper should be ready in about an hour. That should give you plenty of time." Mother walked over to the old lady and put her hand on the woman's forehead. Mrs. Walden was still sleeping.

"She's a little warm. I think I'll brew her some willow bark tea just in case she's getting a fever."

Father left to go outside. He assigned the weed cutting to John and Warren. He and Ben along with Isaac and David removed the boards. They also nailed the shingles on the roof that were coming loose. John and Warren took a rake and scythe and made quick work of cleaning up the yard. William and James picked up loose sticks and then helped Joseph in the barn.

"Supper time," Mother called. Everyone rushed for the cabin. "John, you take this food out to Moses and Jane." Mother handed John a basket that smelled delicious. He hurried out to the wagon.

"Don't worry, John, there'll be plenty for you." Mother laughed. Never-the-less, John hurried anyway. He didn't want to miss any of the scrumptious meal Mother had fixed.

Mary Walden was awake. Mother had made her comfortable, and she was sitting up in her bed with a pretty bed jacket on and a ribbon in her snowy white hair.

"Oh, my, what lovely children," she exclaimed as the children trooped into the house. Mother instructed them to sit down at the table and introduce themselves.

"We have a baby sister, too, but she's out in the wagon," James informed Mrs. Walden.

"I hope she's not alone," Mrs. Walden said worriedly.

"Nope, Moses and Jane are watching her. OUCH! Why did you kick me, David!" James cried, glaring at his older brother.

David looked at Mother and Father for advice. They looked at each other and shrugged.

"Moses and Jane are runaway slaves, Mrs. Walden. We're trying to take them to freedom. If you are uncomfortable with that notion, we'll leave at once," Father said .

"Oh, no. Don't leave," the old woman cried. "I think what you are doing is wonderful. My husband's family had a plantation in

Kentucky. I'm sure they still do. He and I didn't believe in slavery, so we moved to Ohio and brought the slaves he inherited with use. We freed them as soon as we arrived here. They stayed with us a good many years as hired hands, but their children moved west recently with the talk of the gold in California. Please, I'd love to meet Moses and Jane. I want to see the baby, too."

"Warren, please go ask Moses and Jane if they would come inside for a moment."

Warren left. In a minute, he returned with Moses, Jane, and the two babies. Ben came in also, but declined staying. He said he'd keep an eye on the road for any strangers coming.

"Oh, how adorable. I haven't held babies for such a long time and I do love babies. May I please?" Mrs. Walden said as she held out her arms.

Jane and Moses put the babies on the bed. The old lady lovingly touched a soft cheek of each child. She had tears in her eyes.

"You people eat. I'll watch these two for you."

There was scratching at the door. A whimper followed and then a howl.

"Whatever is that?" Mrs. Walden asked in alarm.

"Oh, that's just our dog, T. B. He's used to being with us when we eat. He's not used to being left outside," Joseph explained to their hostess.

"Well, let him in. We always had a dog or two in this house at one time or another, " Mrs. Walden said.

Joseph opened the door, and T. B. bounded in. He walked over to Mrs. Walden and gave her a sniff and then a lick. Content now that he was inside, he turned around three times and laid down next to the bed.

"Now can we sit down and eat before everything gets cold?" Mother asked a little impatiently.

Everyone sat down around the table. Father said the blessing and then Mother passed the dishes around.

Everyone ate a delicious meal while Mary Walden played with the two little ones.

They were just finishing the meal when there was a knock on the door. Before Father could answer it, a young woman rushed into the room. She ran over to Mrs. Walden.

"Oh, Aunt Mary. Are you all right? I'm so sorry that we didn't come to see you after the storm, but we had damage to our house and the store and we were so busy. I feel just terrible that you have been out here hurt and suffering." The young lady stopped talking and hugged her aunt.

Mother and Jane removed the babies from the bed so that Mary could comfort her niece. T. B. Gave a 'whoof' and moved out of the way. He curled himself up by the stone fireplace.

"It's all right, Miranda," Mary said as she patted her niece's blond hair. "These nice people came by and as you can see, I'm fine. I do think, though, that I am going to sell the farm and move into town. I'm a little tired. I'd like to relax and sit and visit with you more often."

"Aunt Mary, you've just made me very happy." Miranda said as she raised her head up. She turned and looked at the Hardings who were still sitting at the table.

"How can I ever thank you for saving my aunt's life? Aunt Mary is like a mother to me and I would have died if anything had happened to her. My husband and I are going to take her back into town to our house where I can take proper care of her. We'll spend the night and take home in the morning."

"You don't have to do that, dear, Helen is coming over tomorrow and I'm sure I'll be fine in a day or so."

"I'm not arguing Aunt Mary Ruth. Helen can help me pack you up in the morning, but you ARE coming to town with me."

In the morning they left Mary Ruth Walden in good hands and went on their way. They took with them some jars of preserves, a ham , and two sacks of potatoes. Miranda told them to stop by the store when they went through town. Each of the children was to get a penny's worth of candy. The children were thrilled.

When they reached the store, the children raced inside. It was hard to decide which candy to choose.

" Hurry children. We must get on our way." Father called from the doorway.

David and Isaac helped their brothers make up their minds. Everyone came out of the store grasping a precious sack of candy in their hands.

The Hardings were on their way once again.

Chapter Nine

Indiana!

The weather continued to be sunny and warm as the wagon ambled its way through southern Ohio. Father pushed everyone a little harder each day to make up for the time that they had lost.

Joseph's birthday was coming in only five more days. He was going to be ten years old. He hoped the older boys wouldn't treat him like a child anymore.

"Mother do you know what is going to happen in five days?" Joseph asked his mother as they were sitting together on the wagon seat.

"Why let me think," Mother said with a thoughtful expression. "Hmm, I can't think of anything special." She said with a twinkle in her eyes.

"Mother." Joseph groaned. "It's my birthday. Don't you remember?"

"Of course I do. I was there, wasn't I?" Mother asked.

"Well, I was wondering what kind of cake you were going to bake for me, and what Father was going to let me do for my day."

"Father is hoping to get to Indiana before your birthday, son. I don't think he's thought about your birthday treat yet. As for a cake, I was thinking of a dried apple spice cake. How does that sound?"

"Perfect," Joseph's tongue could already taste the spicy apples. "and you can tell Father that I want to drive the wagon for a whole day for my treat."

"I'll tell him, Joseph , but that's an awfully long time to sit behind the reins. I know, because I do it everyday." Mother said with a knowing smile.

"I can do it. I'll be ten, won't I?" Joseph asked seriously.

Mother nodded and smiled. Joseph jumped down from the wagon and joined John and Warren who were racing up the road with T.B. .

Father was getting impatient to get across the border into Indiana. He had everyone up before sunrise and they had traveled until it was dark. If he could have figured out a way to travel safely in the dark, he would have kept everyone going well into the night. Joseph shared his Father's impatience. The sooner they got to Indiana, the sooner he could go back to Gran's. The promise he had made to Father and God poked him in the stomach, but he tried to forget it. Three more days and he would be ten.

While they sat around the campfire that night Father looked at the map carefully.

"I think we can cross the border in two days if we continue traveling like we have been." Father said with enthusiasm. "I know it has made for long days, but we just have to get there as soon as possible."

"It's all right, dear." Mother said. "We all know that it's your concern for the winter that is driving you to speed us up. We can do it.

The next day Father had everyone running including the horses and Ellie mooed in protest, but she on trotting down the road. They passed the city of Cincinnati without stopping.

"We're almost to the border." Father said excitedly that night. "We'll have two celebrations in one day, Joseph's birthday and crossing the border. Joseph will be driving the wagon across the border. That is your birthday wish, right, son?"

Joseph smiled and nodded yes eagerly. He could hardly wait until tomorrow came. He couldn't fall asleep, he was so excited.

The next morning was a beautiful, fall day. The air was crisp and cool. The sun shone brightly and there wasn't a cloud in the deep blue sky. Joseph jumped off his pallet and bounced out of the wagon. Mother was fixing hotcakes and molasses. It was his favorite breakfast.

"Hello there birthday boy. Come and eat. You're the first up and by rights should be the first to eat today." Mother said as she handed Joseph a plate filled with steaming cakes.

"Umm, they're good Mother. Thank you."

After breakfast, Joseph got up on the wagon seat and took the reins. Mother sat next to him holding Mary.

"Let's move out, son." Father called. He rode along side the wagon on Belle.

Joseph called "Gee Haw!" and the horses took off down the road. Joseph felt the reins go taunt in his hands and he could feel the movement of the horses. He let up his hold on the reins a bit and willed himself to relax. They had traveled for about three hours when Father came up to the wagon.

"Are you getting tired, son?" He asked. "Mother can take over for awhile if you are."

"No sir." Joseph was about to drop from exhaustion, but he'd never admit it to his Father. "I'm just fine."

Late in the afternoon, Father rode ahead to scout the road. He came galloping back in about ten minutes. "Rachel! Everyone! We're almost to the border! It's just a little ways up the road. Just two more curves and you will cross into Indiana, Joseph!"

Joseph was exhausted but thrilled. He snapped the reins over the horses heads and hurried their pace. Everyone but Mother, Mary, and Joseph ran ahead to wait at the border for Joseph and the wagon.

Even the horses seemed to sense the excitement because they began to go faster. Joseph became scared. The horses were jerking the reins out of his hands. He started to pull back the reins, but the horses were too strong. Sweat broke out on Joseph's forehead. He didn't want to lose control. He couldn't face Father and everyone if the horses became runaways.

"Are you having trouble Joseph?" Mother asked with concern. "It's all right to ask for help if you need it." Mother put Mary in her cradle behind the seat just in case Joseph needed her.

"I'm going to do this myself, Mother." Joseph said through clenched teeth. He stood up on the seat and started pulling with all of his might. He yelled at the horses. He could feel that he was regaining control and the horses were slowing down. By the time the wagon rounded the second curve Joseph had the team under control again. Everyone was standing by a small sign that read "Welcome to Indiana." They were cheering and jumping up and down.

Joseph sat down in the seat and held on to the reins tightly to maintain control. The horses had been spooked once and he didn't think her could regain control a second time. As the wagon crossed the border, Father gave a big yell and threw his hat into the air. Moses and Jane started hugging and kissing each other and the boys danced around the road. Ben sat on his horse and smiled at all the action around him.

Father jumped up on the wagon seat, gave Mother a kiss and Joseph a hug.

"Great driving son. You got the wagon here safe and sound." Joseph smiled and gave Mother a secret wink. She winked back at him and gave him a kiss.

"It's our secret." She whispered into his ear. "You're my hero once again."

That night Mother served everyone a piece of birthday cake. She had made it the night before when everyone was asleep. Everyone enjoyed the special treat except for the birthday boy. He had fallen asleep sitting up. Father carried him to bed and tucked him in.

The family was lighthearted for the next few days. The weather was beautiful. It was perfect Indian Summer weather. The days were warm and sunny and the nights had a slight chill in the air. As they passed through Indianapolis, the family was impressed by the wide streets and numerous businesses along the way. Father would not allow them to stop, however, because he wanted to push on to Uncle Ike's house. According to an Indianapolis merchant Father asked, their destination was only a few days away. That evening, when they camped outside of the city, the wind shifted and the air became cold and damp. Mother made sure that everyone had extra blankets.

"I don't need any of you coming down with a cold or some other sickness now. I won't have time to tend to sick children. Joseph, you bundle up now and help your brothers. Take care of yourself."

"Yes, Mother." Joseph answered. He thought about getting sick again. Maybe then, they'd ship him back home. Then, he thought of how sick he had been with the cholera and decided that there must be another way that wasn't so painful.

They made their way towards Danville the next day. The weather had turned cold, cloudy, and damp. Everyone huddled together in the wagon. No one but Mother, Father, and the older boys saw the small town of Danville as they passed through it. The cold wind blew through the canvas. Joseph couldn't stand it anymore. It was too crowded. He jumped down and walked quickly ahead of the wagon.

"Maybe I can see Uncle Ike's place before anyone else. I want to see this wonderful place that Father was so anxious to get to." Joseph grumbled to himself as he pulled his coat tighter around him and tucked his head into his chin against a wind that was increasing in strength.

He looked ahead and saw Father, Isaac, and David on the horses.

"Father, can I ride with you?"

"Joseph! What are you doing out in this freezing weather?"

"I wanted to get out of that wagon. Mary and James are whining and it is too crowded. Besides, I wanted to get to Ike's first with you."

"Well, Ike's place ought to be about four more miles on this road. If you want to go with us you can, but there'll be no complaining. Do you understand?"

"Yes sir." Joseph said as he climbed on the horse. He settled himself behind Father and wrapped his arms around Father's waist. It was cozy here because Father's body kept the cold from blowing on Joseph.

They rode in silence for the next hour or so. Then Father seemed to get excited. He kicked Belle's flanks and began cantering up the road. David and Isaac felt the excitement and they, too, increased their speed.

"There it is! There's Ike's farm." Father pointed to a fence line about a mile into the distance. Joseph couldn't see much behind Father's back. He could barely see a plumb of smoke rising over the tree line to the left.

"How do you know this is it? You've never seen it before. We could be at someone else's place, Father." Joseph said. He wasn't convinced that Father knew where he was or that this was the right place.

"This is exactly how Ike described his home in the letters he sent. There's the wooded area there and over there is the pond and to the right is his field. The house is hidden behind that grove of trees on the hill. We'll go back and get Mother and the rest now."

They galloped back down the road to the wagon. Mother was huddled on the wagon seat Her eyes were only part visible as she was bundled up in blankets. When she saw the horses she unbundled herself enough to call out.

"Samuel, we must stop for a rest . I'm freezing and the children are hungry."

"There's no need to stop now Rachel. Ike's place is just up the road. We can be there for the noon meal if we keep going."

"How wonderful! Let's go then." Mother snapped the reins and got the horses going at a trot. Mother smiled and settled down in the seat.

Father and Joseph rode ahead again to prepare Ike for the family's arrival. Father turned down a muddy lane that led to the grove of trees on top of the hill. At the top, Joseph saw a large log cabin sitting next to a huge maple tree. The cabin seemed to have many rooms that had been joined together at different times.

"Hello the house!" Father and Joseph called together. "Hello! Is anyone home?"

A tall, thin man came out of the front door of the cabin. He had a long brown beard and a head of bushy brown hair. He was smoking a pipe. Behind him was a short, plump woman with dark brown curls. She was wiping her hands on her white apron.

"Samuel, is that you?" called the man. "It is you by thunder!" Ike Harding ran towards the brother he hadn't seen in ten years.

Father jumped off the horse and embraced his brother. The men hugged the tiny woman who was wiping tears from her eyes.

"We expected you to arrive weeks ago brother. Where have you been? I've been checking out the National Road daily now for the last three weeks. We were getting worried about you."

"It's a long story. I'll tell you all about it over a nice, hot meal in front of a warm fire. First, though, we have to wait for Rachel and the rest of the family."

Joseph felt completely ignored. No one had even noticed him in the happy greetings being exchanged between the adults. He sat on the horse impatiently waiting for Father to say something to him or about him to his Uncle and Aunt. Father continued to ignore him. Joseph hopped down off the horse.

"Ah hmm. Father..." Joseph began.

"There they are!" Father called. He ran towards the wagon that was climbing the hill towards the house. Mother pulled the wagon to a stop and jumped down. She was immediately caught up in hug by her sister and brother-in-law. Mother, too, was crying.

Joseph felt invisible. It seemed like the grownups had forgotten that he and brothers and sister existed. Joseph thought of heading down the road towards Virginia and never looking back. He was getting angrier and angrier by the minute. His parents didn't need him. Now that they were with Ike and his family they didn't need Joseph at all.

The grownups finally stopped hugging and kissing and turned towards the children.

"Ike , I want you and Emma to meet our seven boys and Mary, our baby girl. They're all anxious to get settled on our farm, aren't you children?" Six heads nodded yes. Joseph didn't look at his father.

Ike and Emma gave each of the boys a hug and a handshake. Joseph avoided Aunt Emma's hug by hiding behind Isaac.

"Well, come on into the house. I have plenty of food and we can get started feeding this lot." Emma said as she herded everyone into her spacious cabin.

"Ike, I want to see my land as soon as possible. We need to get it cleared and build a cabin on it as soon as we can. Winter will be here soon."

"Samuel, I've taken care of that for you. Your land is ready for next spring and I've got a house for you to live in this winter. Ben Snodgrass's old house is on the line between our two properties. He's willing to lease it to you for a share of next year's crop. How does that sound?"

"It sounds wonderful. I'm very short of money right now. We had a lot of expenses along the way that we didn't count on. I have only about fifty cents cash money on me at this time. I don't know if we can make it through the winter as it is."

"Well, Emma and I will share our corn crop with you and there's plenty of good hunting in the woods around here. We won't let you starve."

Joseph listened to the conversation between the two men. Things were turning out too well. Joseph felt doomed to stay in this place. Father had no money, but Uncle Ike was helping him out too readily. How was he ever going to get back home? This place was not home. It was a cold, damp, and miserable wilderness.

The next morning the family including Moses and Jane settled in at Ben Snodgrasses's old homestead. It was a small cabin, but it was snug and warm and it had a large loft for the children to sleep in. It also had a small outside shed where Moses and Jane made a home. They were still keeping hidden just in case someone came looking for them. Ben the hired hand, decided to move on west and try his luck in the California gold fields. This gave Joseph an idea.

"Ben, how would like some company on your way west? You know I don't eat much or take up much room. I'll just be traveling with you until I can find someone heading back east to Virginia. What do you say?"

"Sorry Joseph. I can't be worrying about a boy. I'll have enough to worry about with just myself. You should stay here with your family and help them get settled. Your father will need everyone of you to help him get started on his farm." Ben spoke firmly to the young boy.

Joseph walked glumly back to the house muttering to himself about hired help who think they know everything. He didn't see Father come out of the house.

"Joseph, I need your help. You and the boys must help me make a mortar to grind the corn that your Uncle Ike has so generously given us. This corn is going to see us through the long winter ahead so we must get the mortar made so that we can grind the corn into meal. Let's get going."

"Father, is this hard work?" Joseph asked. He was not in the mood for hard work But, he could see he had no choice. Father looked determined.

"Yes, it is Joseph, you and John grab the end of the saw and help me saw a piece of this tree into a four foot length."

Joseph and John sawed at one end of the saw while Father pulled the saw at the other end. Sweat was dripping off of their foreheads before long.

"Father, can we take a break now? We're awfully tired." Joseph begged. John looked at him in disgust.

"Yes. You go help Mother shuck the corn for awhile. I'll get Isaac and David to help me finish up here."

Joseph and John went to help Mother. "You sure give up quick, brother," John grumbled at Joseph. "Now Father thinks I'm a slackered like you."

"Just leave me be, John," Joseph warned his older brother. He hated fighting with his brother but he had just about lost patience with everything and everyone.

John ignored him for the rest of the morning which was fine with Joseph. Mother looked at him with concern but wisely held her tongue.

After the noon meal, Joseph and John were back out in the yard helping Father again.

"Now boys, I want you to watch me carefully. I'm going to get a fire started on the top of this piece of wood. Help me set this stump on its end. Now, after I get the fire started, I want you to remove the ash, but keep the fire going. Make sure that the fire is evenly spaced out so that the fire burns a bowl into the wood. That's where we'll put the corn to grind. Each of you stay on stay on one side. Keep the fire even and steady. Don't forget to empty the ash out. Do you understand what you're to do?

"Yes sir." The boys answered. Father started the fire and got it going evenly across the top of the stump. Then he carefully took the ash out as it burned the wood slowly. Father saved the ashes. Mother would use them later to make soap. Joseph was the first to try to remove the ash. He lost his fire.

"That's all right, son. Just re-light your side with John's fire. Next time remove the ash more slowly."

When he was sure that the boys were doing their task correctly he left them to tend to other chores. Father checked on the boys frequently throughout the long afternoon.

"I'm hot, tired, and smoky, John." Joseph grumbled. "Do you think this dumb, old stump will ever burn down?"

"It's going fast Joseph. You're just too impatient." John said. He was tired of Joseph's whining and fell silent.

Father came back late in the afternoon with a freshly cut sapling that was about seven feet long. Father split the sapling and inserted an iron wedge into it and tied some string around the wedge to hold it in place.

Joseph looked around and saw his little brothers looking on from the porch. He, too, would have found the experience much more interesting if he had been watching Father like James and Warren were doing. Instead, he was standing over a hot, smoky fire choking and sweating.

Finally, Father said the magic words. "It's done boys. You've done a good job. Now, go inside and tell Mother to set the corn shells into hot water. We should be able to grind it tomorrow. You'll need lots of strength for the grinding tomorrow. You'd better get to bed early."

Joseph groaned. He couldn't stand another minute of this whole back breaking, boring process. That night he wrote in his diary:

I am leaving . I am tired. I hate this place.

Mother had everyone up before dawn the next day. "Eat quickly children. Father has chores for all of you. Joseph, you and John are to go outside and help Father as soon as you eat."

Joseph dawdled through breakfast. Maybe if he took long enough, Father would get one of the other boys to help him. He hunched down on his bench trying to be invisible.

"Come on Joseph. Let's go." John called as he put on his coat and went outside.

Joseph dragged himself out the door. There was Father with the mortar and pestle all set up. The pestle was the seven foot sapling with the iron wedge. It was tied to a limb of a tree, which acted as a spring to help raise the pestle up and down. Joseph found out quickly that the spring didn't make the torture of pounding the corn shells that much easier. The spring helped them keep some control of the pestle and they didn't have to hold the weight of the pestle by itself, but Joseph's arms quickly got tired and his body was aching long before the corn was ground into meal. A couple of times the pestle swung loose and caught Joseph off guard. It almost knocked him to the ground. He and John took turns guiding the pestle into the mortar. John poured the corn while Joseph pounded. Then they traded off. He and John pounded corn for half a day. Joseph thought his arms were going to fall off and he would collapse. John seemed to be having a great time. Joseph couldn't understand his older brother at all.

"That's good boys. That should be enough for a few days. Take the corn meal into the house and then clean out the bowl. I will need you to help me repair the barn after you finish that up."

Joseph watched as Father cheerfully headed toward the barn. That's it! I'm finished! He said to himself. I won't do another thing. This place is horrid. We never had to work so hard in Virginia. I hate it here. I've given it a chance, but now I'm going back to live with Gran. I don't care about my promise anymore. Besides, I got cholera. I could have died. God will understand. Joseph reasoned as he crossed the yard.

Determined, Joseph headed off towards the barn to talk with Father. He ignored John's voice calling to him.

"Father, I need to speak to you."

"Yes, Joseph? What is it? I'm very busy and so are you. Can't it wait until this evening?"

"No, it can't. Listen to me Father." Joseph said. Father stopped and looked at Joseph with curiosity. "I'm leaving Father. I hate this place. I hate making corn meal. I hate smoking that wood, and I know whatever else you have in store for me, I'll hate too. You promised me I could go back if I wasn't happy. Well, I'm not happy and I'm going back. If you can't afford to send me, I'll just walk." Joseph finished his tirade and stood facing Father with trembling shoulders. He met his father's look with steely determination.

"I see. I thought that we had settled that issue. Well, I'll take you into town tomorrow. We'll see what we can do. I did promise you, and there's no point in you staying here and making the rest of us miserable. If you are certain about this decision then that's that."

Joseph felt elated and then he felt a letdown. Why didn't Father argue with me like before? I guess they really don't want me to stay. With me gone, they'll have more room and one less mouth to feed. Oh well, I don't need them. I'll be back at Gran's. I'll be at home. Joseph felt much better as he went into the cabin. He watched as Father rode off alone on Belle to Uncle Ike's house.

That night Father made an announcement. "As you all know, Joseph has not been happy since we started our journey, so to keep my promise, I'm going to let him go back to Virginia tomorrow. He has to leave immediately to get back before winter sets in. Moses and Jane are leaving us tomorrow too. Uncle Ike has heard that someone has been asking around town about a black man and his wife. We don't want to take any chances. Moses and Jane will go north towards Canada. If they are separated from us there won't be as much suspicion."

The whole family looked surprised. Then reaction set in.

"Father, how will Joseph get back? He could get hurt. He's not going by himself is he? Joseph, how can you leave us? We're your family. You'll miss us." Each of Joseph's brothers protested the news. Baby Mary cried and would not be hushed by Mother's rocking. Mother looked sad and disappointed. Joseph could not meet her eyes.

The next morning at daylight, Joseph, Father, Moses, Jane, and baby Abraham headed into town in the wagon. Father dropped Moses, Jane, and the baby off at a farmer's house just outside of town. He would take them north with him. They would be helped along the way until they were in a safe place.

Moses and Jane openly cried when they said goodbye. "We can never thank you enough Mr. Samuel. We owe our lives to you and your family. You will be with us in our hearts forever."

"If you can, let us know how you're doing." Father said as he shook Moses's hand. "We'll want to know how you fare. Try to keep in touch. God bless you."

Father and Joseph waved as they rode away. The rest of the trip into town was silent. Joseph felt sad about leaving Moses and Jane. He would miss them. They had become part of the family. He was beginning to have doubts about his own trip too. Maybe he hadn't given Indiana a chance yet. No, he thought, I'll be much happier back in Virginia.

Father parked the wagon next to the general store and said, "Stay here Joseph. I'll be back in a little while." Joseph watched Father carefully as he talked with some men inside the store. They were talking and pointing towards the east. Father pointed toward Joseph and turned back to the men. The men shook their heads and then as Father continued talking they began to nod their heads. One of the men started grinning. Father frowned at him and he stopped grinning, but the man cast a sideways glance at Joseph and smirked.

Father came out of the store with a smile on his face. Three rough looking men followed him. They all approached the wagon. Joseph looked at everyone. The men made him nervous.

"Well, it's all arranged son. These men are heading back east and have agreed to let you go with them provided that you do a few chores along the way. Do you agree? This is the only way you can get back Joseph. Take it or leave it. Hurry up and make up your mind. I have to get back to the farm."

Joseph swallowed. It had been so easy. With a few quick phrases Father had gotten rid of him. He was as good as gone. Well, that's what he wanted wasn't it? It couldn't be worse than grinding corn all day.

"That's fine Father. I'm ready to go." Joseph said as he jumped down off of the wagon seat clutching the bag of his clothes and blanket .

"Well, men I guess that's your answer. Joseph, you obey these men and you'll be fine. Write to us when you get to your grandmother's will you? Your mother will be worried. Goodbye now. Take care of yourself. God bless." Father gave Joseph a hug and got up on the wagon seat. With a wave goodbye, he and the wagon were heading back to the farm.

Joseph felt a huge lump formed the bottom of his throat. His stomach began to ache and he wasn't sure if he was going to cry or throw up. Father had left him right there in the middle of the street with men he didn't even know. He turned towards the men. He had to look up because they were all very tall. They stared back at him with harsh looks on their faces.

"Well, boy. Are you ready to go? We need to get a move on. I hope you're able to work boy 'cause we don't allow no shirkers with us. By the way, I'm Charles, and the other two there are Mark and Thomas. We ride hard and we're in a hurry so let's go."

Joseph nodded and watched as the three men got up on the horses next to them. Charles held out a hand and Joseph climbed on the saddle behind him. He held on for life as the three galloped out of town towards the east.

Realization hit Joseph when they were about a mile out of town. He had left. He had left his Mother and Father. He wouldn't see his brothers or Mary again. He was alone with three strangers who might leave him along the road. Fear knotted Joseph's stomach.

"Please," he gasped. "I'm going to be sick!"

Charles didn't seem to hear him. They all kept pounding down the road. Joseph tugged on Charles's coat causing the man to turn around in the saddle. "What do you want?" Charles asked angrily.

"I need to go to the bushes." Joseph said. He tried to act unconcerned, but his voice trembled.

"Oh, for blasted sakes! Mark! Thomas! Stop." Charles called.

Joseph hid his face in humiliation.

They stopped and Joseph got down. He hurried and was back in the saddle shortly.

"Do you need anything else, boy or can we get on our way?" Charles asked sharply.

Joseph shook his head. They took off and set a steady but fast pace for the rest of the morning. At noon, Joseph felt as if he would never walk again. When they stopped to rest the horses, Joseph almost fell off of the horse. He was sore everywhere and every bone felt like it had been jolted loose. He fell to the ground to rest.

"Not so fast, bud. Go tend to the horses and then get us some firewood. We'll have us a noon meal. Then we can go farther this evening. Hurry up boy!" Charles said and gave Joseph a slight shove which almost sent him sprawling. He dragged himself to tend the horses. He gathered the wood and dropped it in front of the men who were sitting down smoking pipes.

"All right young'n. Rest a minute. Then you can fix us some coffee and heat up this stew. A nice lady fixed it for us this morning. It should be good." Mark chuckled to himself as if he knew a private joke.

Joseph didn't feel like laughing. He was miserable. He wanted to cry, but he wouldn't let these three scoundrels see him weaken. Father wouldn't have left him with these three men, if he'd known what they were going to do. Joseph tried to see Gran and Virginia, but, suddenly, Virginia didn't seem so wonderful anymore. A little cabin with his family crowded into it was picturing itself more and more in his mind.

"Hey, Joe, put a move on it. We don't have all day," Charles called. Joseph came out of his thoughts back to the nightmare that he had gotten himself into. He cooked and then cleaned up. The men took a nap while he was sent to gather grass for the horses. When he returned the men had mounted up and were waiting on him.

"Let's go, boy. You're holding us up." Charlie grabbed him by the collar and heaved him onto the horse. They rode swiftly down roads and lanes until dark settled upon them. They camped under a tree that was next to a pond. The setting was beautiful, but Joseph didn't see it. The men kept him so busy doing chores that he fell asleep sitting up by the fire with his plate still in his hand.

Charles gently took the plate away and laid Joseph down. He covered him up with a blanket. Mark started to laugh, but Charles frowned at him. He put his finger to his lips and Mark and Thomas kept quiet. The next three days passed in a blur for Joseph. He was either hanging on to Charles's waist to keep from falling from the horse, or he was doing chores until he dropped off to sleep in exhaustion. He had already decided he didn't want to continue this trip. He wanted to leave these three lazy men and go back to Mother and Father.

No matter how hard he had to work on the farm, it wasn't as hard as the last four days had been. Gran's house didn't appeal to him anymore either. He wanted to be with his own family in his own bed. He tried to tell Charles that he wanted to go home, but Charles wasn't listening.

"Ah, Charles, I was wondering. Could you take me back to Indiana? I really don't want to go any farther. I've decided that my family needs me, and I really should help them get through the winter. Charles, do you hear me? I want to go back home." Joseph asked. The last sentence came out of Joseph as almost a plea.

Charles grunted but didn't answer. Joseph couldn't see the smile on Charles face or the twinkle in his eye. About an hour later Charles and the other men pulled into a farm. A farmer came out of the barn. "Hey, Charles, I've got those horses that your father asked for. They're down in the west pasture. I'll send my boys to get them."

"No need to do that Mr. Jakes. Joe, you go fetch those horses for us and be quick about it." Charles said as he put Joseph down and pointed him toward the pasture. Joseph groaned and headed toward the field. He found the two horses and brought them back to the men.

"You get on one of them, Joseph, and I'll tie the other one's lead to my saddle," Charles said cheerfully. Joseph blinked. They were giving him a horse to ride of his very own. Mr. Jakes put a saddle on the horse and lifted Joseph up into the saddle. Charles paid the man and they all said goodbye. Charles and the others headed the horses back the way they had come.

Joseph was puzzled. "Charles, where are we going? I thought you were headed east. We're going back west towards Indiana. What's going on?"

"I thought you said that you wanted to go home to your family, or were you storytelling to get out of working?" Charles quizzed Joseph sternly.

"No. I want to get back to Indiana. I just thought you were heading to Virginia."

"We never said exactly where we were going, boy. Just that we were heading east. We've gone as far as we're going. Now, we're going back to our home."

"Your home?" Joseph was beginning to get suspicious of these men. Especially since Mark and Thomas could hardly contain themselves. Mark started to chuckle. Then Thomas began to laugh. Even Charles was grinning.

"What's so funny?" Joseph asked, indignantly. "What's so gol' dern funny?"

"You'll see," was all that Charles would say. During the journey back to Danville, Joseph tried to pry the mystery out of the three men, but none would answer him. They still made him do most of the chores, but he didn't mind so much now that he knew he was getting closer to home. Home! That's where he was heading. His home was where his family was. Not where a tree or a creek stood. Home was his mother tending to Mary or James sitting in his lap. He thought of these things during the seemingly shorter journey back. Then he started to worry. He had made everyone very angry with him. Would they want him back? Or would they banish him? Maybe they wouldn't speak to him for days. John would ignore him for years, but he didn't care! He didn't care. As long as he was near his family, he would be happy. He could take what ever they dished out to him.

Even with the extra horse to pull along, they made it back to Danville in three days. They went through the town without stopping.

Joseph thought this was strange, but the whole journey had been strange. He continued to follow. They rode into Uncle Ike's farm around noon. Uncle Ike waved from the corral and started toward them. Aunt Emma came running out of the house. The three men got off of their horses and gave Aunt Emma a hug and kiss.

"How do you like the horses, Mother?" Charles asked.

Mother? thought Joseph. Mother! All of a sudden it hit Joseph who these men were and what a trick had been played on him. He was sitting there dumbstruck when Charles came up to him.

"Well, little cousin. You ready to get down off of that horse now? Father needs to take a look at him."

Joseph got off silently and stood there stiffly.

"Hey, little cousin, I hope there aren't any hard feelings. Your father thought maybe this trip might open your eyes to what you really wanted. It worked, didn't it? Don't feel so bad. Mark felt the same way you did when we first came here. Father did the same thing to him. That's why he had such a hard time going along with the scheme. He saw himself in your shoes and saw how funny he had been. I sure hope you don't hold it against us. We just wanted you to see that things aren't always as bad as they seem. Friends, Cousin?" Charles said as he extended his hand with a friendly grin on his face.

Joseph shook his cousin's hand and looked up into his face. He realized that Charles was about the same age as David. Mark was a little younger and Thomas was a few years older. They didn't look as old and fearsome as had at the beginning of the trip.

Joseph began to grin to himself at some of the things the boys had made him do.

"One day, cousins, I will get you back for all that work you made me do. You just about killed me while teaching me a lesson. What if you had had to bring my dead broken body back to my family?"

"We made sure you were breathing every night before we turned in, Joseph," Mark said with a laugh. "Besides, you needed some toughening up. Now, the chores on the farm will be easier. You'll see."

"Can I go home, now?" Joseph asked. He was anxious to get his homecoming over. He was scared to face everyone.

"Sure. You just ride on over. We'll get the horse later."

Joseph rode over to his family's cabin with butterflies in his stomach. As he approached the cabin, he saw Mother in the window lighting the lamp. What a wonderful sight, he thought smiling.

James and Warren were in the yard playing with T. B. When they saw Joseph, they began yelling.

"Joseph! Joseph's back! Mother, Father, Joseph's back!" The boys ran to meet their older brother. T. B. howled and barked with glee. Mother came running out of the house. Father came out of the barn with the older boys. Everyone met Joseph as he got down off the horse. There was a lot of hugging ,kissing, crying, and laughter.

"Well, son. How do you feel? I see that you decided to come back. We're happy to see you. Are you planning to stay long?" Father asked with a twinkle in his eye.

"Thank you, Father," Joseph whispered into his father's ear. "This is my home, now. I want to stay with you and my family. I won't be going anywhere unless it's into town. I've journeyed enough for a lifetime. I realize now where my home truly is. It's not a place. It's where you and Mother are and the boys." Mary howled from her cradle. "And Mary, too," Joseph said with a laugh. "I missed you all, and I won't be asking to leave again. I promise."

"Welcome home, son!" Father lifted Joseph up and tossed him into the air. The older boys did the same, The little boys clambered around Father wanting to be thrown, and they were.

CHAPTER 10

Home At Last

During the next few days, Joseph helped Father and the rest of his brothers get ready for the winter ahead. He ground corn meal until his arms ached. He patched the roof and stuffed chinking into the cabin's walls. Father showed him how to mend the fence around the barn. Joseph did everything without one complaint. He was happy to be home, and Mark had been right. He was tough, and he could work at most anything without his muscles getting tired.

At dinner one evening Father make the announcement.

"Tomorrow you boys can go to school. We have most of the chores caught up. You might as well go now. When winter comes, you may not be able to go much, and next spring you won't be able to go at all. I'll need all of you to help me get the crops planted. We'll be building our own cabin next summer if everything works out like I'm hoping it will."

Joseph was elated. He had missed school. But he hadn't wanted to say anything to Father about it. He wasn't about to complain. The other boys moaned and groaned, but Joseph sat with a smile on his face thinking about going to school the next day.

"Hurry, boys, and finish your hominy. You'll be late for school if you don't get a move on." Mother said the next morning as she hustled the children out of the door and down the road.

Joseph walked with a spring to his step. His brothers dragged behind. Joseph enjoyed the mile and a half walk in the cold, sunny morning.

"Come on, boys. We're almost there. I can hear the bell ringing." Joseph said. He ran to the school house with his brothers hurrying behind him. The Silch Schoolhouse sat back off the main road to Danville in the midst of four elm trees. Mr. Cox, the schoolmaster, greeted the boys. "Well, hello, children. You must be the new Harding family that moved into the Snodgrass place. I've been hoping that you would be coming to school. I'm glad to see you and hope that you'll be happy here." Mr. Cox was jovial fellow in his mid twenties who controlled the children with kindness and a sense of humor. Joseph thought he was the best teacher he'd ever had. He was much better that their old teacher, because he made everything so interesting, and he wasn't mean.

Joseph and his brothers were able to go to school for two months that winter. The snows began right before Christmas. They celebrated Christmas with Uncle Ike, Aunt Emma and their cousins. Charles couldn't resist teasing Joseph.

"Hey, Joe. You want to go back east? We'll probably be leaving in April if you do. We sure could use someone to do our chores for us along the way." Charles asked his cousin.

Joseph punched his cousin in the stomach for an answer. "Guess that means no, huh? Oh, well, I just thought I'd ask,."

Charles and his brothers laughingly told the family about Joseph's miserable trip. Joseph grinned good naturedly. He didn't mind. He was used to their teasing by now. Joseph had helped Father hunt for the Christmas turkey. They killed a big one. The feast that the families shared was delicious. Uncle Ike gave each of the children a bag of store bought candy. Aunt Emma had made each of them a new shirt. She made Mary a new dress. Mother cried at her sister-in-law's kindness. Mother had knitted mittens for everyone. Father gave each of the boys a fur hat that he had made from skins that he had collected with Uncle Ike.

In January, the blizzards came and the Harding family was snowed in for days at a time. Mother made sure that the children did lessons daily and Joseph wrote in his diary.

The cabin is real cozy and snug. Sometimes I would like to be by myself, but not very often. We keep busy mending harnesses and fixing tools. Father is building a plow out in the barn. I am helping him as much as I can.

The weather began to clear at the beginning of March, but Joseph couldn't go back to school. Father needed him and the other boys to begin plowing the fields. Mother needed extra help this spring, too, as there was going to be a new baby this summer. Joseph missed going to school, but he kept writing every day, and he was too busy to think about it much.

Father came back from Danville one day in April with great news. He had two letters. One was from Ben and the other was news about Moses and Jane. He also had another letter. He read it first. It was from Mr. Kramer.

I know you took Moses and Jane from me. I can't prove it nor can I do anything about it, but if you or your family ever come back this way, I'll get even with you. I trusted you, and you betrayed that trust. You didn't need to take them. I had already decided not to sell them. I hope you are happy in Indiana.   It was signed Elisha E. Kramer.

"What a confused man," Mother said. "He doesn't seem to know what he believes."

Joseph offered a solution. "Maybe it was us that confused him, Mother. Maybe it will make him think twice the next time he threatens to sell one of his slaves."

"I hope you're right, son. Samuel read the other letters They should be more cheerful than that one," Mother said.

A farmer in northern Michigan had written for Moses and Jane.

We want to thank you, folks, for your kindness to us. We are fine. Abraham is growing into a big boy. We are staying with Mr. Holden right now. After we help him

*with the spring planting, we are going up into Canada
to settle. There is a town up there where many former
slaves are living. They have land and a job for us, as soon
as we can get there. It seems our dreams are truly coming
to pass. We will keep in touch. Mr. Holden is teaching us
to read and write, so that we can write to you ourselves.
God bless you all.*

Love,
Moses and Jane

Mother wiped her eyes as Father read the letter. Joseph felt a lump in his throat, too. Everyone else sniffled a little and grinned.

"It makes it all worthwhile to hear that they made it." Joseph said and expressed the whole family's feelings.

Ben's letter was a real surprise.

*You, folks, won't believe this, but I struck it rich. I found
one of the richest gold mines in this part of California. I'm
buying up land and settling in here. I've met a girl named
Sally and we're going to get married in June. I wish you
could be here. You're the closest thing to a family I have. I
am sending you something to help you get settled in your
new farm. Please accept it with my sincere thanks for all
that you did for me.*

Sincerely,
Ben

Enclosed in the letter was a bank draft for one thousand dollars. Father passed the note around for everyone to see. Mother looked as though she might faint.

Joseph looked at the bank draft and yelled, "Yippee, no more corn meal mush!" Everyone started to laugh. "Well, it's the truth, isn't it?" Joseph asked.

"You're right , son. We can now afford a little more than corn meal mush. We need to give thanks for Ben's generosity and our good fortune, since we have been here."

The family said a prayer. Then Father declared a holiday. Joseph took T. B. and raced down the lane. He ran and ran until he came to a small creek. It had a large elm tree on a hill next to it. Joseph sat down next to the tree and looked out over the creek. He reached out and patted T. B. on the head. He sighed and stretched out. It couldn't get much better than this. Not even in Virginia. Joseph smiled to himself and at everything around him. "Thank you," he said quietly as he looked up at the sunlit sky.

Printed in the United States
88793LV00005B/1-258/A

9 781425 994594